TULIPS AND TROUBLE

PORT DANBY COZY MYSTERY #5

LONDON LOVETT

WILD FOX PRESS

Tulips and Trouble

Copyright © 2018 by London Lovett

All rights reserved.

ISBN-13: 978-1986566049

ISBN-10: 1986566048

CHAPTER 1

I frantically pulled out my tissue to catch the sneeze, my fifth of the morning.

"Gesundheit," Ryder chirped from behind the colorful forest of tulips on the counter.

"Spring is in the air. And in my nose, apparently." With a sniffer as sensitive as mine, it made scientific sense that I'd be prone to allergies. Yet, every spring I got blindsided by the perpetual blizzard of pollen. Especially silly of me, considering I surrounded myself year round with flowers.

I picked up my pruning shears and began trimming the ends of the tulips. "I wonder why it's called hay fever, when it clearly has nothing to do with hay *or* fever."

"I can answer that." Ryder pushed his long bangs back from his forehead. My marvelous, multi-talented shop assistant was a veritable encyclopedia of trivia. "Back in the day—" He paused. "I wonder why we say *back in the day* when there is no specific day to go with it? I'll have to look up the origin of that phrase. Anyway, back some time ago, when people worked the land, runny noses and red eyes were prevalent whenever hay was being harvested."

"That explains the hay part, but what about the fever?"

Ryder tucked three yellow tulips into a slim glass vase. "Good question. Maybe it's because runny noses and red eyes also go with having the flu."

"That sounds about right." I stepped back to look at the tulip arrangements. The bright, waxy blooms ranged in color from deep, rich burgundy to magenta purple and creamy white. "Makes me want to go out and buy a pair of wooden shoes. I don't know what it is about tulips but I've never considered them as part of the flower world. They are so sturdy and solid. They're like nothing else in nature. I'm glad we opted for the Darwin tulip. I think those frilly parrot tulips would have been too much for flower arrangements. They're better in a garden landscape. They just try too hard with their flouncy petals."

Ryder laughed. "Did you just mock the parrot tulip for being an overachiever?"

"I suppose I did. I'm also glad we decided to go with the rainbow of colors instead of just the usual spring favorites. This way people can pick the colors that go with their spring table settings."

Ryder snapped his fingers and pointed at me. "Brilliant."

"Thanks?" I said with a question, not exactly sure how I'd earned the compliment.

"Rainbows. Roy G. Biv," he continued.

I squinted at him. "You've lost me. Who is Roy G. Biv, and why am I brilliant? Other than the obvious reasons, of course."

"Roy G. Biv is not a person. It's a mnemonic device." He tapped his chin as he slipped into a short mind debate, something he did a lot. "Or is it an acronym? Not sure. No, I think it's a mnemonic device."

I blinked at him. "I think my hay fever is worse than I thought because I haven't understood one word since *rainbow*."

Ryder shook himself out of his debate. "Sorry. Roy G. Biv is what people use to remember the colors of the rainbow. Red, orange, yellow, green, blue, indigo, violet." He pointed to the matching tulip as he recited each color. "I'll arrange *a rainbow* of tulips in the front window."

"I love it. It'll attract customers while letting them know that we have a wide variety of colors available." I rounded the work island to grab Kingston's can of treats. I only had to walk to that section of the counter, and the crow started his perch dance, sliding his long, clawed feet along the wooden dowel like a skater on ice. My bird had been extra good all morning while Ryder and I worked on the tulips. He deserved a reward.

Kingston spread his black wings in anticipation of the peanuts. I dropped a handful into his dish and looked out the window. The flowering plum trees that lined Harbor Lane looked like a parade of pink popcorn trees, their fragile blossoms twittering in the on-shore breeze. An incredible display of nature's magnificence, they were almost blinding in their beauty. "Although, any window display, even a rainbow of tulips, is going to have a hard time competing with Harbor Lane's spectacular flowering plum trees." By summer the delicate, papery blooms would be replaced by dark plum foliage.

"Very true." A short laugh followed. "Have you noticed those pink blossoms are like camouflage for the blush pink paint on your shop? If I didn't know it was sitting between the Coffee Hutch and Elsie's Sugar and Spice Bakery, I might have walked right past it."

"I hadn't even thought of that. I suppose we are sort of invisible at the moment."

"Then I'll just have to make the tulip display extra impressive." Ryder was rarely discouraged. At least not when it came to ideas for the shop. His love life was another thing altogether and that was mostly due to my best friend, and flightiest woman in Port Danby, Lola Button. The green-eyed monster had bitten Lola after Ryder started steadily dating Cherise. (Even though Lola refused to admit it.) After the Cherise episode ended with a breakup, I was sure Lola would finally come to her senses and realize that she was smitten with Ryder. She had fallen for him almost instantly, but the second Ryder had shown any interest in return, Lola turned her nose up and away. (Hence, the title 'flightiest woman in Port Danby'.) Now she'd found someone new, but I was holding out hope it wouldn't last. Not for Ryder's sake but for Lola's. And for our friendship. Chuck, the new man, was capital O obnoxious.

"I give you free rein to create your rainbow display."

"Thanks. By the way, boss, can I have a little extra time for lunch today?"

"Of course." I grabbed a broom to sweep up the tulip trimmings. "Any special plans?"

"Just having lunch with my friend, Denise, from high school. I haven't seen her since graduation. We used to be in all the same advanced placement classes. She finished her business degree but discovered soon after that she hated the business world. She wants to pursue art. She's taking a landscape painting class. They are down at Pickford Beach this morning working on oil paintings of the lighthouse."

"How fun. That lighthouse is the perfect model for a painting. Tall, handsome and it doesn't move an inch." The Pickford Lighthouse was a beautiful reminder of the romantic, seafaring past. It could be admired from just about every street in town.

Ryder laughed. "Never thought of that. I guess that does make for a great model."

The goat bell on the door chimed. Elsie, one of the fittest people I knew, was moving unusually slow as she carried in a plate of cupcakes mounded with luscious buttercream.

I breathed in their scent. "I smell lemon and—hmm, I'm not sure. Maybe my allergies are affecting my sense of smell."

"No, your old-fashioned cells are just fine."

Ryder stifled a laugh at Elsie's substitution of old-fashioned for olfactory. I actually thought old-fashioned sounded much more enjoyable.

"Lemon." Elsie pointed to two cakes that were pillowing over the tops of silver wrappers. She moved her fingers to the cakes wrapped in brown parchment cups. "Red velvet. They don't really have a distinct flavor unless that nose of yours can smell the color red. Then it really would be worth a million bucks." She lifted the cupcake as if she was lifting a heavy brick. "I think you'll find that the magic of red velvet is all in the cream cheese frosting, namely *my* cream cheese frosting."

I took hold of the cupcake. It was just the weight I'd expected for a cupcake. "Elsie, what's wrong?"

"Nothing." It was exactly the answer I'd anticipated. Elsie was one of those strong, confident people who never liked to show weakness.

"Nothing? Then why did you just lift this petite, airy cake like it weighed ten pounds? And you walked into the shop like you were moving through tar, when you usually rocket in here like you have tiny thrusters on your shoes."

"It's nothing. A little wrench in my back is all. I was taking some cakes out of the oven and I turned wrong. Did I tell you that my new patio furniture is coming today?"

"Nice topic switch," I noted, wryly. "I thought the cardboard Mr. Darcy fiasco had made it all quiet on the western front and that peace would finally prevail. But it seems I was wrong."

"Stop with that silly Table War stuff." Elsie went to wave her hand but stopped short of an actual wave, which meant she was truly in some pain. "It's just some cute little wicker couches. You know, something to spruce up the store front."

"And something to lure customers away from Lester's highly popular counter-high pub tables."

"Oh, these will lure people my way all right. They are comfy and covered with a charming sunflower printed fabric. Perfect for summer. I just wish everything didn't always happen on the same day. The furniture was supposed to be delivered earlier in the week. Now I'm busy baking for this weekend's big flea market."

"The flea market? Are you going to sell your baked goods?"

"I always sell my cupcakes at the annual flea market. I just hope I can make enough of the them to keep up with the high demand. Red velvet and lemon were my top sellers last year." Her phone beeped. "In fact, that's letting me know the next batch of lemon is done. I'll see you later." She forced a smile to hide the obvious pain she was feeling as she made every effort to hurry out as if she had rocket thrusters on her shoes.

Ryder was peeling down the wrapper on a red velvet cupcake as I turned around. "I'd say she did more than just wrench her back a little."

"I'll say. I'm worried about her. I just wish she could find a good assistant for the bakery. Someone who could meet all of Elsie's high standards."

Ryder licked icing off his finger. "Guess not all shop owners are as lucky as you, boss."

"I know you're being self-deprecating, but you don't know just how true that is, Ryder. You are irreplaceable, even if you're dropping red velvet crumbs all over the floor I just swept."

CHAPTER 2

The morning had started off with a bang. I'd taken five orders for tulip bouquets and one massive order for a June wedding. I pulled a can of root beer out of the mini refrigerator in the office. I kept it stocked with cold sodas and water bottles. The sodas were mostly for Ryder, but after the bustling morning, I decided I'd earned a root beer. The front door opened as I took a few hearty swigs.

"Pink," Lola called from the front of the shop.

I walked out from the office. Lola took notice of the root beer in my hand. "Uh oh, looks like you had an exhausting morning too." Lola's cheeks were red from the sun. She had pulled her hair up into a ponytail. It jutted out from the back of a camouflage trucker's hat. She was wearing a Garth Brooks' t-shirt that went very well with the hat.

Lola climbed onto her favorite stool. Kingston wasted no time in joining the love of his life (which was not me even though I saved him from certain death and provided him with a constant flow of treats), at the work island. The bird landed right in a pile of leaf trimmings, managing to get one stuck on his long talon. He kicked the foot out several times to loosen the leaf from his claw, reminding me of the well-known dance that erupted after one walked out of a public bathroom with toilet paper stuck to a shoe. It took Kingston several tries to lose the leaf. Throughout the entire, somewhat embarrassing event, he didn't take his glassy black eyes off of Lola. But my friend was too steeped in her own thoughts to notice.

"For goodness sake, Lola, acknowledge my bird before he crumples into a broken-hearted lump of black feathers."

Lola reached unenthusiastically over to Kingston and stroked his head. "It's not you, King. It's me. I'm pooped."

"Do you want a root beer?" I held up the can. "It's the perfect drink for a foamy head rush and much needed blood sugar spike."

Lola shook her head. Then a spark of energy pushed her upright. She glanced quickly around the shop.

"If you're looking for Ryder, he's at lunch. With someone named Denise who he knew in high school."

Her posture drooped some. "I wasn't looking for Ryder. And I certainly don't care if he went to lunch with Debbie."

"Denise."

"Whatever." Lola always worked extra hard at showing disinterest when it came to Ryder. She dropped her hand away from Kingston. He looked thoroughly disappointed. "I've spent days picking out the perfect items for my flea market booth, old lamps, vintage glassware, mid century end tables, steamer trunks. You name it, I've got the collectible you're looking for. It took hours to haul the stuff down to the town square."

"You should have asked for help. Ryder and I could have pitched in a few hands." I handed Kingston one of his favorite snacks, a crunchy peanut butter flavored dog treat. It seemed to lift him out of the funk Lola's lack of attention had brought on. He pinched the treat in his long beak and flew back to his perch. It was his favorite time of day in the window. The sun was at just the right angle to send its warming rays through the glass, shrouding his perch in a cozy glow.

Lola hopped off the stool and lifted her hands up high for a yoga stretch. "I had plenty of help. Chuck is still between jobs, so I talked him into helping. He was two hours late, but he made up for it with his brute strength." She folded down to touch her feet.

"Yes, of course. Chuck," I said and realized I sounded just like my mom when I told her I was going to the prom with Troy North. Troy wore a silver hoop in one ear and never brushed his long hair. It was my rebellious phase, a phase that ended quickly when I realized that along with his hair, he also never brushed his teeth.

Lola had met Chuck (whose last name I hadn't even bothered to learn) at a friend's wedding. His dark blond hair was buzzed close to his large head. His square face was rivaled in width by his neck, and he wore t-shirts that were too tight for his thick build. And those were his charming attributes. He was always right about everything, even when he was spectacularly wrong. I was fairly certain it was *that* particularly irritating character trait that kept him from finding a permanent job.

"Jeez, could you be any more obvious about your disapproval, Pink? You're supposed to be my friend. Not my mom."

"You're right. I'll keep my mom tone to myself." I'd spent the last month telling myself not to spend too much time finding fault and distaste for the man because I was certain Lola would tire of him soon. Although, a month was a record for Lola. About two weeks in, I'd considered trying some reverse psychology where I pretended to be impressed and fond of Chuck. Then it dawned on me that my plan was doomed to failure. I just wasn't that good of an actress.

Lola finished her stretch session. "Anyhow, the reason for my sour mood has nothing to do with Chuck. It has to do with Fiona Diggle."

"Fiona Diggle? Who on earth is Fiona Diggle?"

"Fiona is a hunched over, white-haired lady who lives off Culpepper Road in a hundred and fifty-year-old farmhouse. She probably saw the thing being built. She lives with her sister Rhonda, who is equally ancient. Rhonda is off visiting her sons in Arizona. So Fiona decided to clean out the attic of their old farmhouse. She paid a few high school kids to help her drag all the junk down to the flea market. Only it's not junk. It's chandeliers, nineteenth century furniture, porcelain dolls, paintings, there are even a few trunks. No one is going to look at my stuff because they can see it every day in my shop. But shoppers have never been up to Fiona's attic. Apparently not even Fiona. I can't believe how much stuff she hauled out to the market. And she set up right next to me. Every time one of those kids walked past with another attic treasure, my enthusiasm and my shoulders sank in despair."

"Nonsense, you have cool antiques, and thanks to your world traveling parents, most of the things came from some distant, exotic location. In fact, that's the angle you should use. Put labels on your items telling people where they came from. I'm sure you'll get people standing in line and passing Fiona's attic treasures right by."

Lola seemed to pep up from my suggestion. As she mulled over the idea, I leaned down to toss my soda can into the recycling bin under the counter. The door to the shop opened. I popped back up to greet my customer and was pleased to see I had a surprise visitor. Actually, two surprise visitors, Detective Briggs and the oversized, rowdy puppy that was dragging Briggs behind him on a leash.

Whenever it seemed as if Detective James Briggs and I had reached a new level with our friendship, a level that verged on a possible romantic connection, then we both got too busy to follow through on it. I hadn't seen him in several weeks. As always, he was a sight to see. Especially today. Aside from the very cute sidekick, instead of his usual detective suit, Briggs was wearing a dark blue t-shirt, jeans and black boots, signaling that he had a rare day off. He was lead detective for a stretch of coastal cities, and it seemed he was always on duty or being called in to investigate some calamity or other.

"I don't know if you realize this, but you're wearing a puppy at the end of your hand. It suits you very well, by the way."

Briggs' half smile creased his cheek. "Yes, I noticed. And I was hoping you could help me figure out what to do with my new friend."

"I think that's my cue to leave." Lola hopped up and patted the puppy on the head before strolling out. Of course she shot me a secret wink before walking through the door.

I grabbed the can of dog treats, causing Kingston to start his perch dance.

"Not for you, silly crow. It's for our visitor."

The puppy was spotted gray with big floppy ears and a white chest. He looked like a mix of every large dog breed on the official dog breed list. "He's quite a canine concoction." I held up the treat. "Does Dad mind if I give him a goodie?"

"No, I mean yes . . . to the treat. But I'm not Dad. Someone dropped him off in front of the station. They tied him to the lamppost with a rope and stuck a bowl of water nearby. I guess they decided not to keep him and thought that the police station was the place to leave him."

The pup eagerly took the treat from my fingers. I rubbed his head and ears. "He's so cute. Did you think of a name?"

Briggs had extra beard stubble and his longish hair was combed back so that it turned up on the back of his shirt collar. "No, because if I name him, he'll think he belongs to me. And he doesn't. Do you know anyone who wants a big, goofy puppy? So far, he's only inflicted minor damage to my couch and the legs of my kitchen table."

I smothered a laugh behind my fingers. The puppy finished his treat and jumped up on Briggs with massive front paws.

"I think he's already decided that he belongs to you, name or not. I think you look good with a dog."

Ryder came back in from lunch. "A puppy!" He made a beeline for the dog. "Man, what a cool dog. What's his name?"

"Detective Briggs isn't going to name him because he doesn't want to give the pup false hope."

"Do you need a dog?" Briggs asked Ryder. "He's really friendly and only eats certain flavors of furniture."

Ryder laughed. "I'd take him in a heartbeat if I wasn't living at my mom's. She's got three yappy little dogs. I don't think they'd be too happy to see this guy walk through the door." Ryder lifted one of the dog's paws. "According to this, your new buddy is going to be gigantic."

"Yep, that's why I've got to find *him* a new buddy. My house isn't that big."

Ryder patted the pup again. "Too bad. A dog like this is a total girl magnet. Not that a guy like you would need a wingman," Ryder added quickly. "I'm going to start on that window display, boss."

I turned back to Briggs. The puppy was gnawing on the leash. "Are you sure you want to get rid of your big, fuzzy girl magnet?"

"That's what my motorcycle is for," he said, dryly. "And it doesn't chew up my furniture." He glanced over at Ryder, who had set right to work on the tulip display. "Actually, I was hoping you'd have time for a walk down to the beach. I find that the puppy causes less destruction if he's tired."

I smiled politely, keeping up a cool facade, even though my heart had jumped ahead of its usual pace. "I've got time. A walk to the beach would be nice."

CHAPTER 3

*D*etective Briggs and I had danced shyly around each other during the first half of the walk, chatting amicably about innocuous things like how fast the grass in the town square was growing now that spring had returned and the tasty new pickle relish at the marina hot dog stand. It seemed it always took us time to get comfortable with each other after we'd been apart. Although comfortable wasn't really the term. We'd been relaxed with each other almost from the first moment I stumbled into his murder case when Beverly Kent was found dead in her pumpkin patch. Ironically, it seemed that as our relationship turned the corner to something more than a working friendship, we grew less at ease with each other.

It was a little ghoulish to think it, but it seemed we needed a murder in town to help melt the ice again. I decided, instead, to settle for the girl magnet trotting ahead of us with his tail curled high in the air. Animals were always the best ice breakers, and puppies were at the top of the list for conversation starters that led to something other than a discussion about growing grass or tasty relish.

The puppy loped along just a few inches ahead of his floppy ears and on paws that were the size of Elsie's jumbo blueberry muffins. Ryder was right. He was going to be a big dog. "I think you should call him Axl. It's a tough, cool name, fitting for a detective's dog."

"Not keeping the puppy, Lacey. I don't have time for a dog."

The puppy looked back, his tongue dangling out the side of his mouth.

"Look, he knows we're talking about him. And he's smiling at you." The dog turned back around and barked at several gulls perched on the railing of the pier. Seasoned gulls that they were, they barely flinched or twittered a feather. They seemed to understand that the big, slobbering monster was attached to a tether, which was, in turn, attached to a human.

Briggs looked sideways at me. "That wasn't a smile. He's always wearing that same big, goofy expression. Even when he's sleeping. The only time he isn't wearing it is when the leg of my kitchen chair is in his mouth."

I laughed and secretly patted myself on the back for breaking us out of our stilted conversation. "You need to buy him some chew toys. Otherwise, a dog his size could take down a house faster than a swarm of termites. Tom and Gigi carry a lot of dog chew toys in the Corner Market. Maybe Gigi could even knit Axl a sweater. Blue and gold, something with a sort of law enforcement vibe to it." I looked ahead at the dog. "Now that I've used the name in a sentence, it's not working for me. He needs to be a little more edgy looking if he's going to be called Axl."

"Edgy? I had no idea dogs could be edgy. Lacey, I'm not keeping the dog."

"You're just a big ole doggy pooper." I laughed. "Wow, that came out in all kinds of wrong. Harley is a cool name for the dog of a guy with a motorcycle, but the sweater would have to be orange and black then, or—"

"Lacey," Briggs said sharply.

"Right. Sorry. No dog for Detective Briggs and his collection of fine furniture."

"I never said it was fine. I just prefer my kitchen chairs to have four equal legs when I sit down to breakfast."

Just as Ryder had mentioned, a group of five budding artists were sitting in a half circle, a wooden easel in front of each of them as they dragged long brush strokes of oil paint along white canvases. Even from the distance, I could see that several of the painters were highly skilled. It was easy to spot Ryder's friend, Denise, because she was the youngest of the group. She was a pretty girl with dark, curly hair and almond-shaped brown eyes. Maybe a new girl in Ryder's life would shock Lola out of her relationship with Chuck. Or maybe that was just my wishful thinking.

I stared up at the pointy black hat on the top of the spire. The large glass eye of the lantern gazed out over the catwalk and across the rippling emerald sea. "That lighthouse is wonderful on any day, but it always looks especially picturesque when the white spire is contrasted by a bright blue sky."

"I never noticed that, but you're right."

We stopped to let the puppy sniff and roll on the grassy hill leading up to the lighthouse. Briggs lifted his sunglasses to get a better look at the group. "I know that woman up front, the one who seems to be in charge. Ms. Dean used to teach art at Chesterton High."

I looked over at him. "You took art?"

"Yes, why? Is that so hard to believe?"

I shrugged. "Just don't see you with a paint brush and painter's smock. Were you any good?"

"Nope. But I had a choice for my elective class—fine arts with Ms. Dean or home economics with Mrs. Groffett. I figured splashing some paint around a canvas would be way easier than baking muffins."

"And was it?"

"Nope. I should have gone for the muffins. I thought I would just get to hang out, watching the kids who were skilled make pretty pictures, while I messed around with my friends and flirted with cute girls. I almost failed the class and nearly didn't graduate because of Ms. Dean."

"How'd you squeak through?"

"Ms. Dean liked me well enough to let me turn in some extra credit."

"Then we should walk over and say hello to the teacher who saved your high school graduation." I started the hike across the lawn, but Briggs seemed less enthusiastic about the idea.

Fortunately, the puppy decided for him. Without warning, the dog jumped up to its thunder-paws and loped after me, pulling the reluctant detective along behind him.

Not wanting to cut through the group and interrupt the view or their concentration, and, at the same time, *wanting* to avoid any potential calamity that might follow a clumsy, rambunctious puppy into a circle of easels, I carved a path around the art group, a path that took the three of us along the green hedge bordering the lighthouse keeper's garden fence. Marty Tate, the man who had been in charge of the lighthouse for decades was knelt down in front of his powder white house planting a fiery display of orange and yellow snapdragons. It was rare to see Marty out and about. No one seemed to know how old he was, but I'd met Marty on a horse and carriage ride at Christmas and found him to be extraordinarily charming. Seeing him reminded me that he had pictures and stories about the Hawksworth Manor, the infamous site of a century old family murder, that I desperately wanted to see.

"Hello, Mr. Tate," I called as loudly as possible. The constant churn of the sea below and the relentless on-shore breeze swallowed my voice. He didn't notice us until we were in his side view.

Marty looked up from his task. I waved and Briggs said good morning. Marty pulled off his gardener's gloves and moved to stand up. I held up my hand to stop him. "No, please don't stop on our account. We just wanted to say good morning."

Deep lines crisscrossed Marty's forehead and cheeks as he smiled. "Good morning. If you're interested, I'll have the lighthouse open for visitors this weekend."

"Interested?" I said excitedly. "Of course, I am. Thanks so much for letting us know. Happy planting." I turned back to Briggs. "Now the gardening bug has bit me. I'm going to have to plant some colorful perennials at my house."

"James Briggs," a voice called across the way. Briggs sort of froze. He pushed a smile up on his face, a smile that took some concerted effort, before he turned to face his high school teacher.

Ms. Dean had been walking around, commenting on her students' work when she spotted us standing at Marty's gate.

"Ms. Dean." Briggs stepped forward to meet her but was beaten to it by the puppy. The art teacher was slightly taken aback by the outgoing dog but then reached to pet his head. Briggs yanked on the leash to pull the dog back. "My apologies. How are you, Ms. Dean?"

"Please call me Jodie. I'm no longer a teacher, and you're no longer a student." She glanced my direction and nodded.

"Excuse me," Briggs said hastily. "This is my friend, Lacey. She owns Pink's Flowers in town."

We smiled politely at each other. Jodie Dean was a fifty something woman with short, unruly hair that she had trained back with clips. Her shorts and blouse were a few sizes too small, and she kept tugging at the hems. She had a deep, commanding tone, and I could easily picture her in front of a class of twenty high school students instructing them on the proper techniques of sketching.

"James Briggs," Jodie said with a pleasant grin. Her tone indicated that she hadn't lost her fondness for her former student. "You're the second Chesterton Tiger I've seen today. I'm sure you remember your football teammate Dashwood Vanhouten. In fact, when I think back to those days, you two were friends."

Briggs' already perfect posture straightened more at the mention of the name. "Yes, I remember him." He was literally answering through clenched teeth as if it pained him to admit that he knew Dash. And now it seemed they had been more than just two guys on the same team. They'd been friends, according to Jodie Dean. I still hadn't discovered the reason that Briggs hated my neighbor, Dash, and I wasn't sure I would ever know. Or that I wanted to know. I admired and enjoyed the friendship of both men, and I dreaded finding out something that might cause me to dislike one or both of them. So I kept my head in the sand about it and refrained from asking either of them any details. I also worked hard not to bring up one in front of the other. Briggs had an especially hard time hearing about anything that had to do with Dash, and it seemed Jodie Dean's mention of him had just soured the lovely morning walk.

"Your students seem to be doing a wonderful job capturing the romantic mystique of our town's lighthouse," I said quickly, hoping to save the afternoon.

"Thank you." Some short curls popped free of her clips as she turned back to glance at the ring of canvases. "Some better than others. But they are all very dedicated. Letty, the young woman wearing the green smock, is new to the group. She is already showing great promise."

"So you left teaching in a classroom to teach out on location," Briggs said. The puppy had collapsed down at his feet for an impromptu nap.

Jodie laughed. It was a strong, somewhat rehearsed laugh. "I only teach part-time. I also work as an art dealer. Well, I should get back to my students. It was good seeing you again, James." She winked. "I mean *Detective Briggs*."

We turned back toward the marina and toward town. The momentary anger from hearing Dash's name had thankfully vanished. The puppy hopped up from his quick snooze, refreshed and energized. He bounded ahead of the leash, only to quickly be reminded of its existence. But that didn't stop the dog from galloping across the grass like an excited horse.

Briggs shook his head. "Now that's what I call a power nap."

CHAPTER 4

*a*s we headed back, our insistent four-legged tour guide led us toward the activity in the town square. Sellers were arranging their goods and wares for the annual flea market. Mayor Price had used part of the sellers' fees to have a temporary chain link fence constructed around the tables so that the items could be safely set out ahead of the market. This was my first early spring in my new town, so it would be my first Port Danby Flea Market. I was looking forward to it. From what I could see, Fiona Diggle wasn't the only person to haul out attic relics. Rusty toy wagons, bicycles that looked as if they'd seen many miles, faded movie posters, old books and every size and shape and color of glassware cluttered the sellers' tables.

Lola had given a vivid, snippy description of her main competitor, Fiona Diggle, but instead of a craggy, ancient old woman standing behind century old attic finds, a tiny woman with snow white hair, a radiant smile and the cutest frilly yellow work apron was carefully lining some antique dolls up on her table. But Lola had not exaggerated about the attic treasures. I didn't know much about antiques, but it seemed buyers were going to swarm Fiona's collection. She had some truly lovely and aged items.

Lola was bent down, her upper body parallel to the ground as she pushed with all her weight on a large steamer trunk. The cumbersome, unwieldy chest barely moved on the roughly mowed grass. And as she pushed and grunted and turned red in the face, her block-headed boyfriend stood ten feet away in the shade looking at his phone.

Briggs handed me the leash and hurried ahead to help Lola move the trunk.

Lola wiped the sweat off her brow as she thanked Briggs for his help. She shot Chuck an angry scowl and tried, unsuccessfully, to wash it away before I caught it.

"I guess you could have used some extra hands after all," I said as I looked deliberately in Chuck's direction. The oaf was still reading his phone, completely oblivious to everything happening around him.

Lola wriggled slightly from head to toe, trying to assure me she didn't mind that he was in the shade on his phone while she pushed heavy objects in the hot sun. "He's just taking a break."

"So I see." Stop, Lacey, I told myself. Let Lola figure this out on her own. She's an adult. I focused my attention on her collection of antiques and, in particular, a hexagon shaped box when a terse, familiar voice shot across the town square. My shoulders bunched up around my ears.

"Detective Briggs," Mayor Price said even louder after Briggs ignored the first bellow.

Briggs leaned his head closer to me. "The guy never thinks I have a day off."

"Briggs, I need to talk to you." Mayor Price with his angry red complexion and combative demeanor marched toward us.

"I was going to tell you to ignore him, but I'd rather he didn't come over here. He gets even more red faced and belligerent when he sees the irritating flower shop owner," I said quickly.

"I'm sure he wants to ask about parking for the flea market."

"It seems this town can't function without you, Detective Briggs." Our smiling gazes met and locked for a quiet moment. They were silent exchanges that happened occasionally and unexpectedly, and I always looked forward to them. "I'll keep an eye on your new best friend."

The puppy dropped down to rest under the shade of Lola's table. Briggs walked reluctantly toward the mayor. I was relieved not to have to come face to face with the man. Our last meeting was inside the flower shop, when he stopped in to buy Valentine's Day flowers for his wife. I'd bravely forged ahead with a few questions about some of his relatives, namely his great-grandfather Harvard Price and a great aunt named Jane. It seemed Jane Price had acted as Port Danby treasurer for a short time before leaving town suddenly. The current Mayor Price turned beat red and let me know that he didn't appreciate my digging into his family's past. He shut down my inquiry in his usual brusque manner. His abrupt reaction only increased my insatiable need to learn more about the Price family and its long legacy in Port Danby.

Lola circled behind her table and started writing prices on little yellow stickers. "Do you see the veritable antique gold mine happening next door," she muttered quietly.

"She does have some nice things," I admitted. "But so do you." I opened the brass latch on the six sided box. The exterior was covered in embossed leather, rich and dark with age. The brass hinges and latch contrasted nicely with the rustic, yet intricately pressed leather. The interior was lined with green velvet and large pieces of tarnished jewelry. I picked up one brooch, a circle of pearls set in dark yellow gold. The center contained a vivid blue stone. "I thought the box was the treasure, but it's filled with all kinds of goodies." I lifted the brooch up and held it out in the sun to see it sparkle. The sparkle never came.

"Those are what we in the antique jewelry world call *paste*. Pretty worthless, even with the aged patina and vintage design. Your first instinct was right. The box is the treasure. It's an early nineteenth-century jewelry box that my mom found in Spain. It's been sitting in the shop for two years. People look at it. And even though I'm selling it with the custom jewelry, there just doesn't seem to be a big demand for leather jewelry boxes."

I rubbed my fingers over the geometric designs etched into the leather. "That's a shame. It's interesting that the previous owner purchased a jewelry box that took a great deal of skill and time to make and then filled it with as you say 'paste'."

"No, it's not that unusual. Even back then, people didn't leave their good stuff in the jewelry box. Too obvious for a thief. They kept valuable jewels hidden in unexpected places, like humidors on a bookshelf or even in the children's nursery, in toys or dolls." Lola lifted the box to show me the bottom and pointed out a tiny black latch. "Here's another trick." She pulled open the latch and a small trap door opened, reminding me of the battery compartment on a television remote. Only this compartment held a brass skeleton key. "A lot of old trunks and boxes have secret keys."

"See, add little stories like that to your antiques and people will walk right past Fiona's display."

"I suppose I could add little note cards on some of the more interesting items."

There was an empty fold out table next to Lola's. "Why don't you spread your things out too," I suggested. "You've still got all this space."

"No, that is Elsie's table. She asked me to save her a spot. She sells her cupcakes at the flea market."

"Yes, she mentioned that to me. I just hope she can manage with a sore back."

"Guess it's good she's so tough."

Chuck somehow managed to make loud foot stomps on the grass. His arrival startled the puppy out of his nap, but instead of jumping up to greet the new person, the dog stayed under the table. Animals were always excellent judges of human character. It seemed Briggs' puppy was no exception.

"Hey, Lo-lo," Chuck crooned. "I'm going to head out. Troy and Ben are heading over to Chesterton for some burgers. And I'm bored of moving all this old, dusty junk around."

"That's fine," Lola said with forced politeness. "I wouldn't mind if you brought me back a burger. I'm going to be stuck here all day setting up."

"Yeah, I would." He rubbed his square jaw. "But I'm not making a special trip back here just to bring you a burger. I'll call you later." He walked away, leaving behind a strained quiet between Lola and me.

A few more seconds of silence passed before Lola broke it. "I know what you're thinking, but he did help me move a lot of stuff out here."

"I wasn't thinking anything." I added an innocent head shake. "Nah, that's not true. I was thinking all kinds of things, but I know you don't want to hear any of it so I'll keep it locked up." I used the skeleton key on my lips and then handed it back to her.

"You're right. I don't want to hear it so just keep that key turned tight."

"Yep. Sealed lips. I've got to get back to the shop. Let me know if you need any help. Or I could send my extremely chivalrous, polite and handsome shop assistant. I know he would love to lend a hand."

"You're sure interested in my love life considering you and Detective Heartbreak over there fidget around each other like two lovesick penguins just waiting for the other to make the first move. Now run along. I've got note cards to write." Lola waved me on, not giving me a chance to respond. Not that I had a response.

Briggs finished his conversation with Mayor Price. The mayor of my town refused to even glance my direction, which was more than fine by me. It was a nice, beautiful morning, and I didn't need his dark scowl to cast shade on it.

When the puppy caught sight of Briggs, he bounded toward him, nearly knocking him off his feet with a big, wet hello as if they'd been separated by oceans and years instead of yards and minutes.

Briggs tried not to return the exuberance but in the end broke down and gave the dog a hearty rub and hug. He caught me admiring the moment of affection and straightened abruptly. He shot me one of those 'don't even say it' looks. It seemed none of my friends wanted to hear my opinions or thoughts this morning, so I would keep them to myself. In the end, I was sure everything would turn out just as it should . . . and just as I predicted.

CHAPTER 5

*A*fter seeing Marty Tate add cheer to his garden with colorful, velvety stocks of snapdragons, I decided my front yard could use a dose of cheer too. Since the spring equinox had brought our fair little town closer to the sun, it meant longer hours of light. The warm spring day had stretched into a lazy, cool spring evening with the bonus of a few extra hours of daylight. It was the perfect time to fill my garden with color.

Ryder and I had brainstormed some ideas while we cleaned up for the day. In the end, I'd decided on purple asters, which were demure and understated and the perfect partner for ostentatious, showy pink cosmos. And not to overwhelm the eye with hot colors, I purchased a flat of papery white sweet alyssum. They would add a layer of peace and serenity to the flowery montage.

Kingston's talons click-clacked along the roof shingles as he watched me from above. For Nevermore, kneeling down anywhere was an invitation for the cat to curl up around my feet. He occasionally took the time to bat at my heels or the hem of my shirt with his paw. Couch potato that he was, that was Nevermore's idea of play.

I slipped an aster plant out of its plastic pot, ran my trowel edge through its bound roots to loosen them and lowered the purple cluster into its new home in my front garden. Heavy dog breathing temporarily pulled Nevermore up to his feet, but the cat dropped back to its haunches when he realized it was only Dash's dog, Captain. Captain sat next to me and stared with interest into the holes I'd dug for the flowers.

"He's probably hidden a few bones in your garden," Dash said from behind.

I twisted around and used the side of my hand to shade my eyes from the deep orange setting sun. Most of Dash's features were blotted out by the bright light, but his tall, impressive physique made for a nice silhouette against the dusky sky.

"I figured he was more interested in long lost rawhides than in my transplanting technique."

Realizing the setting sun was too harsh for me to stare up at him, Dash circled around and sat himself on the bottom step of my porch. Nevermore decided the porch steps looked more comfortable than my feet and joined Dash. The cat circled between his legs and rubbed his head against the rough fabric of Dash's jeans.

We were still months from summer, but Dash's blond hair was streaked with pale yellow and his skin was already a rich brown tan, two delightful consequences from his job fixing boats in the marina. His skin tone made his green eyes stand out like vibrant jewels.

I scooted my rubber knee pad over to the next set of holes and pulled the flat of sweet alyssum closer.

"I suppose I should plant some flowers in front of my house now that the porch is finished. It's just I have so many other things to do in that wreck of a house, taking time to spruce up the garden seems sort of silly." Dash was one of those rare men who was perpetually positive and happy. But his mood seemed to be off this evening.

"Everything all right?" I asked. "Or is that house just getting to you? It is a lot of work, and with a full-time job on the boats, I imagine you don't have much free time these days."

"Yeah, it's the house and the lack of free time." He sighed, a sound I rarely heard from him. "I noticed you had some spare time today."

I sat back and looked up at him, not sure where he was heading with his comment.

Dash reached down and pretended to be busy scratching Nevermore's ears.

I jammed my trowel into the dirt and picked up a plant. "I did have a very nice walk down to the lighthouse this morning, if that's what you're referring to." I couldn't help but answer with a touch of snip. It was a natural response to his somewhat judgmental tone.

"I didn't mean anything by it, Lacey. It's just I saw you with Briggs, and I guess I was feeling a little jealous. You guys looked as if you were having a good time. And what's with the big dog? Don't tell me Briggs finally grew a human heart and got himself a dog."

I dropped the alyssum into the hole and sat back to give him a stern look.

He lifted his hands in surrender. "Sorry, that's two for two. I probably should have stayed at home with my sour mood. I think I just had too much sun today."

"So now you're blaming the beautiful weather for your grumpiness?"

"I guess so." He stood up from the porch.

I pulled off my gardening gloves. "It's all right, Dash. Everyone lands in a bad mood. I'm just not used to seeing you in one. I'm sure being out on the water in the hot sun all day would wear down anyone's mood."

"Thanks for being understanding. And I promise, next time I'll stay in my wreck of a house and growl at the peeling plaster and warped floor boards instead of you." As he spoke, a convertible Mustang filled with high school kids zipped up Myrtle Place to the Hawksworth Manor. "How are you doing with solving the Hawksworth murder mystery?" The new topic had erased some of his frown. And mine.

"I haven't had much time lately, but after my last visit to the library, I'm convinced that the murders had something to do with the Hawksworth shipyard."

"You mean the shipyard that never happened?"

"Yes. And it never happened because Mayor Price, Harvard, not Harlan, squashed the whole idea in court. It had to be devastating for Hawksworth. I have no idea how the events are connected, but I'm working on it."

His smile had returned. It was extra white in his suntanned face. "I'm sure you'll figure it out. You seem to have a knack for finding killers." The last turn in topic inadvertently took us back to my friendship with Briggs.

I worked up a few seconds of courage to question him before he walked away. I figured Dash was far more likely to talk than Briggs, who was always more reserved.

"I met Ms. Dean, your high school art teacher, on the walk."

Dash scrubbed his hair back with his fingers. "Yeah, I ran into her on the pier."

"She mentioned that you and James were friends in high school."

A small muscle flexed in his cheek, reminding me of Briggs whenever Dash's name was brought up. He nodded without looking directly at me.

"Exactly what happened between you two?" The question shot out before I could stop it.

Dash paused and seemed to be considering his answer. A

thread of adrenaline pumped through me as it seemed I was finally going to have the mystery solved. Then his answer came, and it couldn't have been more cryptic.

"Let's just say there were some mistakes and some misunderstandings and a good deal of regret."

"I see. That tells me absolutely nothing, but like I've told James and now you, I enjoy your company and I enjoy his company. So whatever happened between you, it has nothing to do with me."

"Good point. And I'm glad you enjoy my company because I enjoy yours." He patted Captain's head to push him along. "I'll see you later, Lacey."

"Have a good night, Dash. And don't give those warped floor boards too hard of a time."

CHAPTER 6

"How does she keep this place so spotless?" I asked Lola as we walked into Franki's Diner. The chrome counters were polished to a blinding gleam and the red vinyl seats were so shiny they looked wet. And all the while, dozens of plates of corn beef hash, gooey cheese omelets and syrup coated pancake towers were being pushed through the cook's window and carried out to the diners. Lola and I stepped into the line waiting for the next table.

Lola rubbed her stomach. "Darn, there's a wait. I knew I should have had a pre-breakfast breakfast this morning."

I looked at the old fashioned analog clock on the wall. "It's six in the morning. What time is pre-breakfast?"

"The second I get up. I'm always hungry as a bear in the morning. Especially after moving antiques the day before."

Franki swirled past her anxious, hungry line of customers and handed each of us a small paper plate with a fresh sample of coffee cake. "While you're waiting. It's my new recipe." She stopped and pushed her piled high bee-hive, the hairdo she wore for the diner, back off her forehead. "Just a warning for those of you with lactose intolerance, it contains both sour cream and cream cheese." With that announcement, she dashed off toward the dining room.

Lola pushed her coffee cake sample into her mouth. "Hmm, now I want more. That was just a tease."

I was still marveling at the woman. Franki was raising four teenagers on her own while running an incredibly successful business. And she still found time to treat waiting diners to a special cake sample. "If there were a contest for Port Danby Super Woman, I think it would be a toss-up between Elsie and Franki. They both have popular food businesses that need a revolving door just to keep up with the flow of traffic, yet their floors, kitchens and counters are spotless. If I make a peanut butter and jelly sandwich, I practically have to drag the garden hose inside to rinse off the kitchen counter."

Lola hadn't heard a word I said. She was busy staring at my sample. "Are you going to eat that?"

I could have been a good, generous friend and handed her the sample, but it smelled delicious, like a sugary confection of cinnamon and love. And Franki had mentioned something about sour cream *and* cream cheese. Two of my favorite forms of *cream*. I picked it up and pushed it into my mouth. "Ye—p," I stuttered over the bite of cake. "What time do you have to open up the booth at the flea market?"

"There is no set time. You can set your own hours, but I'm heading straight over after I eat." She stretched up to get a glance into the dining room and grunted as she dropped back to her feet. "Everyone is just taking their sweet time eating this morning."

"You really are hungry." I was feeling a twinge of guilt for not handing over my cake sample. Then again, it *was* delicious and probably worth the loss of good karma points.

"I didn't have dinner last night. Chuck was going to pick me up and take me to dinner but . . ." She stopped, seemingly deciding not to tell me how the story ended. She knew she didn't need to provide me with any more reason to dislike the man.

"I'm going to assume that you didn't eat because you didn't go to dinner because Chuck never showed up."

"Assume what you want." Lola lifted her chin and looked away. "I think I'm going to get the French toast with a side of bacon."

"He's not worth it, Lola. You'll see that soon enough." Sometimes it was just too hard to hold my tongue, a trait, or perhaps weakness, I'd obviously inherited from my mother.

Lola swung around to respond but was cut short by the restaurant door opening behind us. "You just don't know him like I do," she blurted and turned back toward the dining room.

"Hey, boss." Ryder forced a smile as he looked past me at Lola, who was busy pretending not to see him. The pretty artist, Denise, was with him, which may or may not have been the reason for Lola's rude behavior. Two more of the artists were with them.

"Everyone, this is the wonderful flower shop owner I was telling you about. Lacey, this is my friend from high school, Denise."

Ryder moved on with his introductions to a thirty something woman with baby fine blonde hair and skin so fair it was almost transparent. I'd taken special note of the woman the day before, not so much for her fairness but because her canvas showed she was an extraordinary artist. "This is her artist friend, Scarlett," Ryder continued. The tips of her long, white fingers were stained with color.

"Letty, actually. That's what most people call me."

Ryder nodded. "Right. Letty. I forgot."

As the nickname was being discussed, the fourth member of their party, a forty something woman, looked irritated by it all. She seemed agitated as if she'd had too much coffee, but something told me it had more to do with Letty and her cute nickname. She stuck her hand out. "Hello, Greta Bailey, I understand you have hyperosmia. Very interesting. I suppose that makes you sort of like a human version of a bloodhound."

I sucked in a breath. "Uh, yes, I hadn't really thought of myself that way, but I guess I can see the analogy."

Sweet little Denise gave me an apologetic head tilt. I winked back to assure her I wasn't upset. She moved closer. "Ryder thinks you are a wonderful boss. He loves working at the shop."

"I'm lucky to have him," I grinned up at Ryder, but his attention had been diverted to my rude breakfast mate.

"Hey, Lola, thought you'd be out selling antiques already," Ryder said cheerily.

"Can't very well stand out there all day if I haven't eaten," Lola answered back coldly.

I knew Ryder was hurt by her response, but he was always smooth. He brushed it off and went right back to a conversation with his artist friends. I joined in their chat, deciding Lola needed a cooling off period. Or maybe I needed it. Either way, I wasn't in the mood to talk to her after her needlessly curt response to Ryder.

"What time are you setting up your easels?" I asked. "Are you hoping to get out there at the same time to catch the sun at the same angle?"

"That was the plan," Letty answered. "But we might have to make some adjustments. The lighthouse keeper mentioned to us that he'd have the lighthouse open for tours today. I guess he does it every year during the annual flea market."

"I suppose it would be hard to paint the lighthouse with people walking in and out of it all day."

"We're going to give it our best shot," Denise said happily. Denise was sweet and cute, while my best friend was working hard to be the exact opposite of sweet and cute. It seemed my secret wish to see Ryder and Lola together was becoming more and more of a long shot.

Letty reached into her purse and checked her phone. "Jodie

says we can postpone the session until late morning." She dropped her phone back into her purse and snapped her fingers. "Darn, I guess that means we'll have to spend the next few hours shopping at the flea market." She raised her hand and Denise high-fived her.

"You two have fun," Greta said sharply. "I'm already behind on my painting. I'm going to set up my easel anyhow. There's no law that says I have to wait for Jodie."

It was easy to tell that Letty and Denise were not terribly disappointed that Greta wouldn't be joining them for their flea market excursion.

Lola grabbed my arm. "Let's go. Franki's got our table."

"Enjoy your breakfast and I'll see you in a few hours, Ryder." I followed Lola, who was practically running to the table. I slid into the booth and Lola slid in across from me.

"What are you going to have, Pink?" she asked.

I felt my brow arch up and my nostrils flare just a touch before I lifted the menu up as a wall between us. It was going to be a quiet breakfast.

CHAPTER 7

*A*fter about twenty *chilly* minutes at the breakfast table, Lola finally broke through the ice and my frosty exterior with a funny story about her parents losing each other at the Heathrow Airport in London. Apparently her mom had handed her dad her phone to hold while she went into the restroom. Somehow, her dad got swept up in a big crowd and carried away from the restroom exit. It was a cute, funny story, and a wise choice for Lola. By the time we were paying the check, we were back to our old selves. I just had to come to terms with the fact that Lola was dating a goober and passing up her chance with Prince Charming. (Apparently, I wasn't very close to those terms yet.)

I had a few hours before I needed to open the flower shop. Since I was up and about and stuffed full with eggs and hash browns, I decided a stroll through the flea market would be the perfect end to the morning.

The morning sun, still curtained by a few clouds, was holding its warmth for later in the day. I zipped up my sweatshirt and stuck my hands in the pockets. The flea market was already in full swing by the time we reached the town square. Just as Lola had predicted, cute little Fiona Diggle with her collection of attic treasures was already the darling of the flea market. She had tucked herself in a puffy winter coat and fur trimmed hat for the cold coastal morning, which only made her look more adorable. She looked a little overwhelmed by the attention her things had garnered.

Lola grunted in disappointment as she set her stuff down behind her table. Her frown disappeared instantly as her own table was swarmed by a group of customers. She set right to work answering an array of questions from two women interested in an art deco style lamp.

I headed through the maze of tables and makeshift booths searching for anything that might be fun for the shop or the house. My new garden flowers had looked drippy and dreary this morning as I walked out of the house, but it was early and cold and they were still recovering from the shock of being transplanted in the garden. I was sure they'd look beautiful once their roots had taken hold. I decided some hanging baskets of color on the porch would be the perfect addition for spring.

I walked over to a table that was overflowing with baskets. Kate Yardley, the owner of the Mod Frock, was searching through the same baskets. She was wearing a dark blue, double breasted pea coat with big brass buttons and extra wide lapels. I admired Kate's unique sense of style, and this morning's ensemble made me feel extra frumpy in my sweatshirt and jeans. I pushed my out of control curls back behind my ears as if that would somehow make me look more stylish. Kate was the one person who could make me feel self-conscious about my appearance, something I normally didn't worry about because as my mom always reminded me, you can only work with what nature gave you. She'd always amend that pearl of wisdom with her usual 'unless, of course, you are rich enough for plastic surgery, or even better, married to a plastic surgeon'. My mom was never subtle with her *mom hints*. This morning I would have just settled for a better wardrobe choice.

"Morning," Kate said faintly, almost as if she'd rather I didn't even hear her greeting. She was not the friendliest person in town, at least not to me. She did however go out of her way to greet my neighbor Dash whenever he strolled past her shop. They had dated at some point in the past, before I lived in Port Danby. I didn't know Kate well, but I'd gotten the sense that she fancied a restart on their relationship. Seeing her brought back to mind the odd conversation I'd had with Dash while planting flowers. He was sure out of sorts and not at all his usual self.

"Morning, Kate." I reached for a natural woven seagrass basket. Kate's hand, bedecked with sparkling rings and glittering bangles, landed on the same basket. We both forced a grin, but neither of us dropped our hold on the basket.

"Don't worry, girls," the woman behind the table chirruped. She leaned down and pulled a second seagrass basket out from under the table. "I've got two, so you can each have one."

It seemed the prospect of having the same basket didn't appeal to either of us. We both politely declined. I decided to move on to the next table where a robust looking man with a handlebar moustache was selling kitchenware items.

The man's cheeks were already red, and the day had just started. But he was quite the exuberant seller. His thick hand shot toward me. "How do you do? I'm Roger Brooking and welcome to my table." He waved his hand over the collection of iron frying pans, meat grinders, industrial sized spatulas and other kitchen implements that looked as if they needed an instruction guide. "As you might have guessed, I'm a retired chef. I worked in some of the best restaurants on the west coast before settling in Mayfield. Can I interest you in a silicone steaming lid?" He picked up a rubbery round disc with a handle and tiny holes.

"I'm not sure I need one of those." I walked to the corner of the table to admire a set of knives sitting in a wooden block. The sleek handles were inlaid with crystal white mother-of-pearl.

"Aren't those magnificent?" he asked.

"They are beautiful. Probably a little too elegant for my usual cooking session of scrambled eggs and macaroni and cheese."

"I can let you have them for two hundred dollars."

"Ooh, yes, definitely too elegant for my kitchen. I'm afraid I'm more of a ten dollar knife chef."

The ends of his moustache had been twisted into tight curls, reminding me of a villain in a silent movie. The curled tips rocked back and forth as he spoke. "Ah, so you're a tomato lumberjack?"

I laughed. "Did you just say a tomato lumberjack?"

He picked up a wood handled carving knife. "Yep, it's a term I use for people who use cheap, dull knives." He ran the knife back and forth over an invisible vegetable, using the technique that lumberjacks used before the invention of chainsaws.

"Ah, I see. Yes, I'm a tomato lumberjack. Only I rarely wear flannel in the kitchen."

His laugh was boisterous, like his personality. I could easily picture him with his tall white chef's hat barking orders at his sous chefs to cut onions and check the soufflés in the oven. "I like you —" he paused for me to fill in my name.

"Lacey."

"Huh, I would have taken you more for a Linda or Susan."

"Nope, I'm pretty sure it's Lacey."

His laugh startled a baby awake in a nearby stroller. The mother didn't look pleased.

"Yep, I like you. In fact, just for you, I'm going to take twenty-five dollars off those knives. That way you can stop torturing those poor tomatoes."

I looked longingly at the knives again. "They are lovely, but I think I'll have to pass for now. Unless the guilt of being a tomato abuser wears me down, then I might be back. But it's been wonderful talking to you, Roger."

"You too, Linda. Take care."

I headed back to Lola's table with my new, apparently more fitting name and a heavy sense that I'd been mistreating vegetables for years. Lola was busy with a customer, busy enough that I was sure she wouldn't notice if I took a quick glance at Fiona's items.

Ryder's friend, Denise, and her friend, Letty, were at the table. They had been joined by Jodie Dean, the art teacher. Letty was holding one of Fiona's porcelain dolls in her arm. I didn't know much about antique dolls, but the Victorian clothing and painted porcelain face were in excellent shape, as if the doll had sat untouched in some corner of the attic for decades. I browsed the colorful glass vases Fiona had lined up at the end of the table. She had good prices on all of them, and they would be perfect for bouquets.

"Those are so pretty," Denise noted over my shoulder as she waited for Letty to decide whether or not to buy an oil painting of a mountain landscape.

"Yes, they'll make for nice custom arrangements."

"It's only a hundred dollars." Letty held up the painting and chirped to Jodie, who shrugged her indifference.

"But the ornate frame itself must be worth that," Letty continued.

Denise moved closer and lowered her voice. "Letty's work is getting noticed in collectors' circles. She sold a painting for five grand. Unlike the rest of us, she can be a little freer with her money."

"Wow, good for her. She must be very talented."

Letty held the painting up higher to read the name in the corner. She waited for Fiona to be distracted by another customer. "I think this might be original," Letty whispered, looking again to Jodie for her expertise. "It might be worth a lot of money."

Jodie's sharp laugh startled Letty. "Scarlett, if you like the painting, buy it. But I doubt art collectors will be knocking down your door soon. It's just a simple landscape, and frankly the proportions aren't very good."

Letty held it up again. "I rather like it. Those purple lupines on the valley floor are spectacular. I'm buying it," she said confidently.

Jodie made a puffed sound through her teeth. "It's your money, Letty."

Letty looked at it again. "You're right. I'll put it back."

As I considered which glass vases to buy, Kate Yardley walked brusquely by with not one but both of the seagrass baskets on her arm. Apparently she'd changed her mind when she found I wasn't interested in them. Naturally, now I wanted a seagrass basket or at least some cool basket. I made the decision to head back over to the basket table once I paid for the vases. I settled on two tall aqua glass containers that reminded me of tall milkshake glasses. The top rims were rippled like the edge of a wide-brimmed, flouncy hat. What I especially liked was that the glass had hundreds of tiny air bubbles.

While I waited to pay for my vases, Lola caught sight of me standing in Fiona's line and mouthed the word 'traitor' to me. I returned an apologetic shrug and paid for the vases. They were going to be perfect for tulips.

CHAPTER 8

*I*t took some organization but I managed to get three large baskets and two glass vases back to the shop in one piece. Fortunately, Lester was outside the Coffee Hutch wiping off tables when I trudged past with my arms full of flea market finds.

"Let me get the door for you, Lacey." He tossed his cleaning cloth over his shoulder and hurried over to my shop door.

"Thanks so much, Lester. That was perfect timing."

He opened the door and then reached out for the vases. I was clutching one in each hand, which wouldn't have been so bad if the three baskets hanging from my arms weren't cutting off my circulation.

I handed him the vases. "Thank you so much. I was starting to lose feeling in my fingers."

The bell and voices had brought Ryder out from the office. He was carrying the last piece of a sandwich. "Hey, boss, you should have texted. I would have come out and helped you."

"I would have texted, only my hands were too full. I got a little carried away. There were so many nice things out there."

Ryder pushed in the last bite of sandwich and picked up the vases. "These are great. The aqua colored glass will be perfect for yellow and white tulips."

"I agree."

"Where's Kingston?" Lester asked as he noticed the empty perch.

"I went to breakfast early with Lola and then to the flea market. I'll be getting the cold feathered shoulder from him this evening."

"Spoiled bird." Lester chuckled as he headed to the door. He looked in the direction of Elsie's bakery and turned back. "My sister is baking herself silly over there and all with a sore back. Did you see the furniture she bought?" He rolled his eyes.

"I saw it on my way in today. She probably wouldn't have bought it if a certain coffee shop owner hadn't adorned his sidewalk with fun pub furniture."

"I came up with the idea because my tables were getting old and wobbly."

Ryder and I exchanged 'oh sure' glances.

"It's not my fault that my ideas are brilliant," Lester added as he walked out of the shop. Before the door shut completely, Denise stepped inside. Ryder released a low sigh, and it wasn't a 'there's my dream girl' sigh. It was more of a 'here she is again' sound.

"Hello, Lacey, I hope you don't mind me dropping in to see Ryder." Denise practically sang as she spoke. She stopped and her admiring gaze swept around the shop. "This place is awesome, just like Ryder said."

"Thank you, Denise. That's always nice to hear." I winked at Ryder. "And you too."

"We're waiting for the crowd to thin out near the lighthouse," Denise continued as she fingered some of the tulips. She turned her white smile to Ryder. "It's such a beautiful day, I thought you might like to get a hot dog with me down at the marina."

Ryder did a great job at trying to look disappointed. "Oh wow, Denise. I just had my lunch break. Otherwise, that would have been fun. But I'm working on a window display, so the rest of my afternoon is booked up." Ryder knew well that I would let him take a walk to the beach with Denise if he wanted, but apparently he wasn't interested.

I got to work putting together an order I had for a birthday brunch. Ryder walked to the other side of the shop where we kept vases and containers on tall metal shelves. Denise followed him over to that side.

"Oh, I didn't tell you," Denise said excitedly to Ryder's back while he picked out the vases for his display. "Letty just got an offer to showcase some of her art at a big show in Boston."

"That's cool," Ryder said quietly.

"Cool isn't the word. It's amazing," Denise continued unabated by Ryder's obvious disinterest. "Greta is so mad. I thought steam would start shooting out of her nostrils. I feel kind of bad for her though. She's been working so hard and for so long to get noticed in the art world, then Letty just skips in and picks up a brush and ta-da, she's a star."

"I guess that would get in anybody's craw," I interjected. Ryder was only nodding and giving one syllable responses. He pushed my metal rolling cart across the store filled with the things he needed for his tulip rainbow display. The full focus on his task finally led Denise to conclude that he was busy.

"I guess I'll let you get back to work, Ryder," she said, sounding less cheery than when she'd walked in.

Ryder was not capable of being a complete boob. He finally stopped and pushed his hair off his face as he gifted Denise with his winning smile. "Yeah, hey, I'm sorry I couldn't go on that walk. Don't forget to try the new pickle relish. It's really tasty."

"I will." The perk returned to Denise's step as she waved and walked out of the shop.

A few minutes of silence followed while I trimmed white roses for the brunch. "You could have gone for a walk, Ryder."

Ryder turned around and sat on the edge of the window. "I know. It's just after hanging out with her for a day, I remembered why I kind of stopped doing stuff with her in high school. She's nice and always in a good mood, but she's sort of needy." His phone buzzed. He pulled it out of his pocket and held it up. "As in texting ten seconds after she saw me in the flower shop." He texted something back and put the phone in his pocket.

"I can see where that might be off-putting." I stepped back to admire my arrangement of white roses and mini yellow calla lilies. It was perfect for a spring brunch table. I reached for another white rose to start on the second bouquet when someone yelled out as if in great distress.

Ryder popped up out of the window and looked my direction with wide eyes. "I think that came from next door at the bakery."

I dropped my shears and raced for the door. Ryder was right behind me. Lester rushed past the shop, his face as white as his hair. We found Elsie on her side on one of the wicker settees. She was groaning in pain and looked even paler than her brother.

Lester and I reached her side. Lester dropped to his knees with a grunt. He was a retired fireman. I had no doubt he'd seen many injuries and accidents, but it was always different when someone near and dear to you was suffering.

He took Elsie's hand. "Sis, what happened?"

Elsie drew in several deep breaths, but her words came out weak and shaky. "I dropped my phone and went to get it." She closed her eyes. Speaking was taking all her energy.

Ryder spotted the phone beneath the settee and pulled it out. "I've got your phone."

"So your back is out?" Lester asked.

Elsie lifted her arm slowly and raised up her thumb.

"Should we call an ambulance?" Ryder asked.

Elsie took another deep breath and tried to sit up. "Ow!" she howled and relaxed back onto the sunflower cushions. "I think I'll just stay right here for the rest of spring."

Lester looked up at me. "She's stubborn and I know she won't go to the doctor. This has happened before. I need to get her home to her special heating pads."

"I'll wait here with her while you close up your shop and get your car, Les."

"Right." Lester hurried away.

"What should I do?" Ryder asked.

"Go inside the bakery and turn out the lights. Check that all the ovens are off," Elsie squeaked through a tight jaw. It seemed every movement hurt. "My keys and purse are in the office."

Ryder went into the bakery to lock it up.

Elsie moaned but this time it was from disappointment more than pain. "I was just about to take all the cupcakes to the flea market. Dozens of cakes ready to be sold to cupcake hungry buyers. What timing."

"I'll take them down there for you, Elsie. Ryder can finish up work at the flower shop."

Elsie lifted her head. The incident had knocked her toffee and gray hair free from its tight bun. "Would you really do that?"

"Of course, Elsie. You'd do the same for me."

"I would, Pink. I've got everything laid out on the counter, including the cash box. The cupcakes in the refrigerator are for tomorrow, but I would never expect you to work both days."

"Why not? Tomorrow's Sunday and I would probably just be spending it cleaning the house. I will take care of the cupcake stand."

Lester's car pulled up to the curb.

"You just go home and put on those special heating pads."

"You're the best, Pink. Thanks."

CHAPTER 9

I handed off the last of the lemon cupcakes to a little girl whose smile nearly split her freckled face in two. There were still a dozen red velvet cupcakes left, but I had no doubt they'd be gone in the next hour. I felt so terrible for poor Elsie, knowing there was nothing I could do to help her feel better. I was relieved that I could at least put her mind at ease by selling her cupcakes. She'd worked so hard and through back pain to get the cakes ready for the flea market. It would have been a shame not to sell them.

Lola dropped some money into her cash box. She had sold quite a few items, including the leather jewelry box and the large steamer trunk. In my spare moments, between cupcake customers, the jewelry box and trunk had given me an idea. Lola walked over and took another bite of the cupcake she'd been working on between sales.

"Lola, I was thinking about a trunk I saw in the gardener's shed up at the Hawksworth Manor. I don't know if you've ever been in to see the artifacts—"

A dry laugh nearly made Lola spit out the cupcake. "Please, I'd hardly call them artifacts. Just a bunch of old junk. I'm not sure why they bothered to preserve the stuff."

"Maybe because the town makes good money from tourists interested in seeing the items left behind by a murdered family. And yes—as I said that out loud, it sounds macabre that tourists come to Port Danby and pay money to see that stuff, but anyhow, I was getting to a question that I'm hoping my antique expert friend can answer."

"Fire away but I have to warn you, I haven't been inside that gardener's shed *museum*—" She pulled out her air quotes. "Since the twelfth grade when Scott Vicente and I hid in there to—" Her cheeks darkened beneath the rosy color she'd earned from standing in the sun all morning. "You get the point."

"No, actually, I don't." I placed an elbow on my forearm and pushed my fingers under my chin to show great interest. "Perhaps you should elaborate about your visit to the gardener's shed."

"Funny, funny friend. You're lucky you provided me with a red velvet cupcake, otherwise I might have stomped angrily off to my own table." She touched her table. "Over here. Five inches away. What's the question?"

"I was thinking about the jewelry box and the secret key compartment. There's an old storage chest in the shed that has never been opened. The lock wouldn't budge when I tried to open it. Do you think a trunk like that might have a secret key compartment like the jewelry box?"

"It's very likely. Of course, there's no guarantee that the key is still stored in the compartment."

"It's worth a look anyhow."

"You're still trying to solve the Hawksworth murders?"

"Sure, why not? It's interesting."

"I suppose." We stood and watched Fiona sell her last doll. Jodie

Dean, the art teacher, came up to Fiona's table and looked through the paintings that were stacked against an end table.

"Excuse me," she said, rather urgently. "Where is that mountain landscape in the antique gold frame?" she asked Fiona. I found it rather curious that she'd come back for that painting after she'd scoffed at the idea when Letty considered buying it.

Fiona shuffled around her table to the front where the paintings were stacked. She looked worn out from the long day. From what I could tell, she had sold more than half of her attic treasures.

Fiona moved a few of the paintings around and then put her hands to her mouth. "Why, I nearly forgot, that pretty young woman with the blonde hair and fair skin came back and bought it a few hours ago."

Jodie looked more than a little upset about missing out on the painting, a painting she'd told Letty not to buy. Maybe she was angry that her advice had been ignored, but somehow, I doubted it. Jodie had mentioned to Briggs that she was an art dealer. It seemed she might have discovered that the painting was valuable after all.

"Interesting," I muttered to myself.

Lola looked over at me. "What's interesting? Oh, I see. The detective and his new side kick. You know, Detective Briggs is even more appealing with a big puppy at his side."

I spun around and was more than a touch pleased to see Briggs and the puppy walking through the crowd. He was dressed for work in his shirt and tie.

"I knew you would decide to keep him. And you brought him to work with you," I called as he reached us.

The dog tried to pull Briggs past the table, toward the picnic benches in the town square where people were eating, but he managed to stop him. It took him a few tries to get the dog to sit, but he finally managed it.

Briggs reached up and loosened his tie. "I didn't decide to keep him, and I had to bring him to work. I was afraid I'd come home to complete and utter destruction if I left him there alone. Last night he got up and decided to eat all the books on the bottom shelf of my extremely small library, a library that's even smaller now that all my World War I and II books have been eaten."

"Perfect, so he's a war history buff too."

Briggs scanned the table of cupcakes. "Have you decided on a career switch?"

"No, I'm helping out Elsie. She hurt her back." I picked up a cupcake. "Red velvet?"

"No, thanks. I haven't had my lunch yet. Actually, that's not true. I *had* a lunch, a delicious looking turkey and cheddar on rye from the Corner Market. I left it on my desk when Hilda needed my help out front—"

I put my hand up. "I think I can finish that story in my head." I'd been very unsupportive, teasing him and insisting he should keep the dog. It was time to be a better friend. "Briggs, puppies are total scoundrels. It's what makes them so darn cute and at the same time troublesome. But they give back more than they take. That's all I can say about it. I wish I had more pearls of wisdom for you, but he's a cute, sweet animal. If you're determined not to keep him, I'm sure someone else would love to take him home. You might need to put up some flyers."

"Yes, Hilda is making some up for me right now." Then, without realizing it, he beamed rather fondly down at the dog. "Turns out he loves to sit for the camera." He pulled out his phone and showed me pictures, just like a proud parent. He swiped over to one. "In this one he's wearing his goofy smile."

I held back my grin. "I suppose it's good you'll have a few pictures of the puppy on your phone to remember him once he's found his permanent home."

Briggs closed out the pictures abruptly. "I know what you're trying to do, and it's not going to work."

I blinked innocently at him. "Why, Detective Briggs, I have no idea what you're talking about. Now if you'll excuse me, I've got cupcake customers."

CHAPTER 10

$\mathcal{F}$lea market shoppers preferred morning for their excursions. By late afternoon, the town square was nearly empty. Although that might have been more due to the ominous cluster of rain clouds that had moved in over the shore. A rambunctious wind had tagged along with the dark sky. I'd discovered very quickly that weather in Port Danby could change in an instant.

After smashing it down several times on her head, Lola yanked off the straw fedora she'd worn all day to protect her from the sun. She turned her face up to the sky. "I thought that storm wasn't due until Monday."

I pulled my phone out. "Looks like the little rain icon moved to Sunday." I ran my thumb down the screen. "From midnight until four in the morning to be exact."

Lola scoffed at that. "Exact. Sure, it tells you the hours to expect the rain, but there should be a little banner on the bottom that says, 'unless you're in Port Danby, then this prediction could change without warning'. I'm going to have to take some of this stuff back to the shop, or it'll be ruined in the rain." Some of the other sellers were doing the same thing. No one looked too happy about the prospect of dragging everything back home just to bring it all back out for Sunday.

"I guess the fence was helpful, but what you really needed was a tent."

Lola snapped her fingers. "Great idea. I'm going to ask Mayor Price to do that next year."

"Just don't tell him it was my idea, or he'll respond with a resounding *no*."

"I can't understand why he doesn't like you. I mean, what's not to like? You even spend your day selling cupcakes for friends."

"I know, right? By the way, I was thinking of going over to Elsie's tonight to cook her dinner. Why don't you come along? It'll be a girls' night."

"I think I've got a date." Lola glanced around. "Chuck is supposed to be on his way to help me take this stuff back to the shop." Her smile appeared. "There he is."

Chuck galumphed toward us, looking none too happy about being summoned to move furniture again. He was such a thick, brute of a man, I didn't notice Ryder behind him until Ryder tilted his head past Chuck's blockhead to look for me.

I waved to him. "*My* helper is coming too," I said to Lola, who was quickly doing a finger comb through her red curls trying to erase the hat marks. "And frankly, I think mine is much cuter than yours," I added just before Chuck reached her table, giving her no time to mount a defense. Not that there was one.

"Babe," Chuck grumbled the word that was normally used as a term of endearment. Coming from him, it just sounded cringe-worthy. But he had my friend stupefied with his big, intrusive presence. "I thought I was done hauling this old junk around," he added to his 'babe' greeting.

Ryder reached my table. "I've got everything closed up for the night, boss. I took in an order for a large family Easter dinner. Mostly tulips and lilies."

"Perfect. I'll have to order some more lilies then."

The conversation at the next table grew a little louder and less 'babe-ish' with each passing moment. Ryder and I were pretending not to notice, but we weren't doing a great job of it. Ryder looked everywhere but to the right where Lola was having to convince Chuck to help her move things back to the shop to avoid the rain.

"I guess the artists finished up at the lighthouse," Ryder said as his gaze swept down to the coastline. "Can't blame them though, those clouds look pretty solid with rain." His eyes swept toward Lola and Chuck and then returned back to me. "Do you need help carrying these trays back?"

"No, I'm fine."

"It's your dusty old junk, I don't see why I have to waste my Saturday night moving it," Chuck growled.

Ryder bit down and tightened his jaw as he looked their direction. I lightly touched his arm, startling him out of his angry trance.

"She needs to find this out on her own," I said quietly to him.

He nodded but it was so tight, his head barely moved. I'd never seen Ryder so mad, but Chuck was just one of those rotten people who could make even the coolest people lose their cool. I know I was losing mine.

I'd been so occupied trying to keep the lid on Ryder, I hadn't noticed that things had escalated at Lola's table.

"What are you doing?" Lola asked sharply.

Our attention snapped that direction at the urgent sound of Lola's voice. Chuck had lifted up a small, midcentury end table. He held it up over his big, square head. "You want me to move the stuff, then I'll move it." Without warning, Chuck spun around and heaved the poor, innocent end table against a nearby tree. Its long, frail legs snapped like toothpicks and it clattered to the ground in pieces. Lola burst into tears.

I was still in a state of shock as Ryder closed the gap between him and Chuck. My stomach twittered with worried nerves. Chuck was two inches taller and outweighed Ryder by about fifty pounds, although some of that was blubber and rocks for brains. That didn't stop Ryder from acting the gallant and stepping in before the villain did any more damage. Or worse. I hurried over to Lola's side and put my arm around her as she sobbed quietly into her hands.

"This is none of your business," Chuck thundered at Ryder.

Ryder wasn't the least bit intimidated. He stepped closer, toe to toe, with the brute. "Lola no longer needs your help. You need to leave."

Chuck's nostrils flared. I quickly searched around for something I could clobber him with if he tried to hurt Ryder. I marveled at how confidently Ryder kept his posture as he stared straight up into Chuck's face. Lola stopped crying, and it seemed she was marveling right along with me. Even with a little twinkle in her tear-glossed eyes.

Chuck didn't move, but he didn't retreat either. He was also too stupid to come up with any counterargument. A long game of chicken ensued, but neither man looked away.

Chuck finally broke it off. "Whatever. I've got places to be." He stormed off like an angry Frankenstein.

I looked over at Lola. The twinkles had grown into shiny stars. Ryder deserved the stars.

Ryder's rigid posture finally relaxed. He spun around. "Are you all right?"

Lola swallowed and nodded but couldn't find her tongue.

Ryder didn't quite know how to react to her silence, so he busied himself by heading to the tree to pick up what was left of the end table.

"I know this isn't the time or place to say I told you so, but I told you so," I said in a near whisper. "And that man right there is as close as any guy can get to Prince Charming."

"He was so brave," Lola finally spoke. It was a shaky, weak version of the real thing. "He didn't even flinch. Did you see how he didn't even flinch?"

"I sure did." I was smiling on the inside, feeling pretty pleased with myself and my matchmaking skills (even though Ryder had really done it all on his own), when Denise came virtually skipping across the town square.

"Ryder," she called moments before reaching him.

Lola's shoulders dropped. "That's the problem. He *is* Prince Charming, and every woman is lined up with their glass slippers."

"But he's only looking for one Cinderella." I decided not to tell her that my intuition told me that she was the girl with the right glass slipper because it was only that, intuition. It was possible Ryder had already given up on Lola. She had certainly gone out of her way to ignore him and be snippy with him to let him know that she was not interested.

Denise helped Ryder pick up a few pieces of furniture and looked rather confused about it all as she walked back to the booth with the broken table legs. Denise's big brown eyes circled back to the tree. "I know the wind kicked up pretty hard this afternoon, but it's wild to think that it tossed a table all the way over there." It seemed Ryder had come up with a somewhat plausible reason for the broken table, saving Lola the embarrassment of the real story.

"I guess you're done painting for the day," I said, trying to take the focus off the flying end table.

"Actually, we are going to meet at dusk to practice painting a stormy sky. A turbulent sky like the one out over the water can evoke so much more emotion than a clear blue one. It's great for creating a dark, moody painting." Denise reached over and wrapped a proprietary arm around Ryder's. He stiffened some in response. So did Lola, but for different reasons. "I came over here to invite Ryder for dinner afterward. We're going to paint until dark and then head over to Franki's Diner for some chili and cornbread." She pouted her lips. "But the big stinker says he can't make it."

Ryder flashed me a friend's secret look, which I could easily read. It went right along with the complaints he had mentioned earlier in the flower shop.

"Yeah, sorry. Wish you'd asked me earlier, Denise. I've got plans."

Denise cleared away the pout and hugged him. "I'll catch you tomorrow then. Have fun with your other *plans*."

"Yep, catch ya later," he said as she walked away.

Ryder turned back to Lola. "I'll help you carry this stuff back to the antique store."

Lola patted her hat back on her head. "No, that's all right. You've got plans. Besides, Pink has already volunteered to help me. You go ahead, Ryder. And thanks for your help."

I stared over at the side of Lola's face hard enough to turn her to stone or a pillar of salt or something along those lines. And she knew darn well I was looking at her. She could probably even sense that I wanted to lift my fist and knuckle punch her right in the arm. (Which I didn't do, but I really wanted to.)

Ryder stuttered over his words for a second. "Oh, right, O.K. no problem." He pointed behind him with his thumb. "I'll just get going on those plans. See you Monday, boss." His long legs carried him quickly away.

The second he was out of earshot, I followed through on my knuckle punch.

"Ouch," Lola reached up and rubbed her arm. "Why did you do that?"

"And thanks for your help?" I repeated her highly inadequate thank you. "He stepped in front of that hulking, furniture throwing cave man to protect you and that was the best you could do? And why didn't you let him help you with the furniture?"

Lola pulled an empty milk crate out from under the table and started stacking in the old books she had out on display. "You heard him. He has plans."

"That's what he told Denise because he didn't want to hang out with her."

Lola stopped and took a deep breath. "Oh, Pink, Ryder's too good for me. I'll just get swept up in it all. Then weeks later he'll be sending me the 'I was thinking we should date other people' text. I can't deal with that kind of disappointment."

"You're wrong. Ryder isn't like that."

She turned to me. "No? He broke it off with his last girlfriend the second things got too serious."

"That's because he likes you."

She waved her hand dismissively. "That's because he doesn't know me. End of Ryder discussion. What are we cooking for Elsie tonight?"

"You're going to go with me?"

"Well, I'm pretty sure I no longer have a date, so yeah, I'd like to tag along if you don't mind."

"Not at all. Girls' night it is then."

CHAPTER 11

$\mathcal{I}$t was a relief to see Elsie with color in her cheeks and not writhing in pain. She sat on her kitchen chair with a heating pad tied around her back and belly. Even from the chair, she was still giving orders on how much salt and onion to use for the enchiladas.

"You know, if you dip those corn tortillas in the sauce first, they'll roll up without breaking," Elsie said as she sipped a glass of white wine.

I already knew the pre-dipped tortilla trick but pretended that she had just alerted me to something profound. I rolled the tortilla around the mound of cheese and onions. "You're right. It does work better."

"See. Told you so." Her words were slightly stretched, but she had only had one glass of wine. Then it occurred to me that the *magical* heating pads weren't working alone.

I glanced back at her just as she took another sip, only it turned into more of a gulp.

"Elsie, just out of curiosity, did you take some pain medication?"

"Me? Never. Wait. Maybe I did. I think Lester gave me something. I was in terrible pain." She took another drink. "But I'm feeling much better." She went to put the glass down on the nearby counter but came up a few inches short. I dropped the tortilla in the sauce and lunged for the wine glass, managing to grab it by the stem before it shattered on the kitchen floor.

"Oops," Elsie said on a comically delayed reaction.

"Oops indeed." I put the glass in the sink. "I'm thinking the wine with the pain pills might have been a mistake."

The doorbell rang.

I wiped my hands on the apron Elsie'd lent me. "That's Lola. She was stopping off to buy some ice cream." I went to the door.

Lola held up two bags. "Couldn't decide between cookies and cream and rocky road, so I bought both. Then I grabbed a vanilla caramel swirl for good measure," she added as she swept past me into the house. "No rain yet but I can feel it in the air."

I followed her to the kitchen.

"How are you feeling, Elsie?" Lola asked.

"Real good," Elsie said, nice and slow. "Really, really good."

Lola never missed anything. She flicked a questioning brow my direction. "Why is she talking like the way molasses sounds coming out of the jar?"

I lifted the wine glass. "I didn't realize she'd had a pain pill before I poured her a glass of wine."

"Ah, that makes sense." Lola put the ice cream in the freezer. "The way I'm feeling, I can probably down all this ice cream in one sitting."

"The way she's feeling?" Elsie asked. "What did I miss? Darn this back of mine."

Lola finished loading in the ice cream and then leaned into the refrigerator for the bottle of wine. "It won't be as good without the pain pills, but I could really use a glass tonight."

"Oh boy, now I really need to hear what happened," Elsie said. "Lola rarely drinks wine. What did I miss?"

I stayed quiet, deciding it was Lola's story to tell. Of course, if she left out key details, I'd be right behind with finishing touches of my own.

Lola poured herself a glass of wine and leaned against the kitchen counter to sip it. "Nothing much except Chuck is a big, slobbering idiot."

"Well, Lola," Elsie piped up, "we already knew that."

Lola looked slightly hurt. "Then why didn't you guys tell me? I thought you were my friends."

I jammed the next enchilada into the tray and turned to her. "Are you kidding me with that right now? I've done everything except wear a great big sign that said 'Chuck is a big, slobbering idiot'."

Lola sank back against the counter. "All right, I'll give you that. You did try to warn me on numerous occasions. That jerk actually broke an end table."

"What a jerk," Elsie repeated. Her words were shortening up. Instead of molasses she was talking like maple syrup. I was sure she'd sleep well tonight regardless, which was probably the best way to heal a bad back.

I finished rolling the last enchilada and put the casserole dish in the oven. Then I turned to Lola. "Are you going to finish your story?"

The heavily painted faces of the Kiss band stared up at me from her black t-shirt as Lola blinked her brown eyes at me. She acted like she didn't have the slightest clue what I was talking about.

"I covered the horrid moment when Chuck destroyed the end table, leading me to the conclusion that he was a jerk."

Elsie clapped. "Good for you. How did you get rid of him? Did you tell him to bug off?"

I crossed my arms. "Yes, Lola, how did you get rid of Chuck?"

Lola harrumphed loudly. "O.K. Ryder stepped up to Chuck and told him to leave." She pushed her hand to her chest and looked at me. "My heart was pounding. I was so worried that Ryder was going to get hurt. But he just stood there with his broad shoulders firm and his manly jaw set tight."

Elsie clapped again. The habit was new and funny. The usually strident, in control Elsie had been replaced by her much giddier doppelganger. I was enjoying this lighter version. "Good for Ryder. That boy is a peach." She pointed at Lola . . . sort of. "You should not let that boy slip away. A guy like that, like my Hank, comes around only once in a lifetime, and sometimes, never in a lifetime." Elsie drifted off for a second into some daydream that was making her grin like a schoolgirl. "Did I tell you Hank insisted he would hop on the next plane home when Lester called to tell him I'd hurt my back? He's all the way in Scotland right now. He was just going to drop everything and come home. But I told him I'd be up and about by tomorrow selling cupcakes and that it would be a wasted trip home. Still, he's such a dear."

"You're a lucky woman, Elsie," I said. "But I think you better let me sell those cupcakes tomorrow. If you don't let your back heal completely, you're just going to find yourself right back where you were today."

"Pink's right, Elsie. We'll make sure the rest of your cupcakes get sold."

"Oh, I can't ask that of you girls again," Elsie insisted.

"Yes you can. That's what friends are for." I picked up the dinner preparation dishes to wash. "Are the Sunday cupcakes in the bakery refrigerator?"

"Yes, four trays. Are you sure? It probably would be good for me to rest another day."

"Absolutely," I said. "I'm looking forward to it. It's fun to watch people's faces when they take their first bite of an Elsie cupcake."

The wine had really gotten to her. It was the first time I'd ever seen Elsie get teary eyed. "You two are the best." She sniffled once and took a deep breath. "But, Lola, I'm never going to talk to you again if you let that Ryder slip away."

"Boy, that went in a direction I wasn't expecting," Lola quipped. She took a sip of wine. "Elsie, first I have to have him before I can even worry about him slipping away."

CHAPTER 12

*S*ince a few hours of cold rain had left the trees laden with big water drops, Kingston took one flight around the neighborhood for his Sunday morning 'drive through the country' and was pecking at the front window seconds later. I opened the front door. He marched past me, on clickety-clacking talons, his wings tucked back and his beak out straight, almost as if he couldn't believe I'd let him out in the first place. He hopped back onto the perch in his cage and spun around to skewer me with an angry glare.

"I apologize, your highness. I forgot you don't like to get your feathers wet. Just so you know, members of your species are not usually quite so fussy. They also don't get warm, hard-boiled eggs every Sunday morning. I know that shocks you but it's true. Just ask a few of them next time you're out pretending to be a bird."

I tossed a few of his favorite treats in his cage and locked him in. I'd decided long ago it went against nature to leave a bird free in the house with a cat on the prowl. Not that Nevermore did much prowling, but I didn't want to take the chance.

Nevermore was deeply involved in a paw licking session as I grabbed my purse and phone and headed out the door. The storm had blown through as a short, temperamental burst of rain, wind and thunder. But by dawn, the sky had cleared of clouds and the wind had exhausted itself to a light breeze. I zipped up my sweatshirt and climbed into my car.

Lola would already have been at the flea market for several hours. She had to bring a few things back out to the town square, but after more wine, cheese enchiladas and a disgraceful amount of ice cream, she decided she would leave most of the things behind in the shop. She'd concluded that if it didn't sell on the first day, then it probably wouldn't be flying off the shelf on day two. And whatever she had left at the end of the day had to be hauled back to the shop. I, on the other hand, had only four trays of cupcakes to transport and set up at Elsie's table. And I was certain I wouldn't have anything left but the empty trays at the end of the day.

Heavy jewels of water sparkled like rainbow diamonds on the lush grass of the Graystone Cemetery, making it far more cheery than a graveyard had a right to be. The entire town, shop fronts, sidewalks, streets and all, looked clean and freshly washed as I headed down Harbor Lane to the bakery. I parked out front.

Lester had taken the time to cover Elsie's brand new wicker furniture with the tarp covers she'd purchased. He had stopped by for a plate of enchiladas and to check on his sister before heading off to a poker game with his friends. He'd mentioned that he was only going to open the Coffee Hutch for two hours so he could go back to Elsie's and take care of her.

I pulled the keys Elsie had given me out of my pocket and pushed them into the lock. On clear days, especially Sundays when the town was all but deserted, noise and voices carried easily. I heard the clamor of the people and activity down in the town square. For a brief second, I was sure I heard a short burst of a police siren. I might very well have imagined it.

I walked inside the bakery and took four trips out to the car with trays of cupcakes. Elsie had them packed perfectly with little plastic domes to protect the luscious mountain of frosting on each cake. I placed two trays side-by-side in the trunk and the other two securely on the back seat. Then I locked up and drove down to the town square.

In my quest for the most convenient parking spot, one that would give me the shortest, simplest route to the cupcake table, I failed to notice that Officer Chinmoor's squad car was parked by the Pickford lighthouse until the spinning red light caught my attention.

I searched around and saw the person I was looking for. Briggs was wearing the gunmetal gray suit that always looked good with his complexion. (Wow, my mind went straight to that superfluous detail before I could stop it. Nevertheless, it was a very good color on him.)

Briggs was talking to, of all people, Marty Tate. Marty was bundled in a thick gray sweater, red scarf and bright yellow rain hat, even though there wasn't a cloud in the sky. I rushed to carry the first tray to the table, hoping Lola could quickly fill me in on whatever excitement I'd missed while waiting for my bird to firm up his Sunday agenda.

Lola was busy with a customer as I reached the table. It seemed she was going to be occupied for a few minutes, so I raced back and grabbed the next tray. Briggs was talking to someone wearing a fuzz trimmed coat, the hood pulled up over their head. The person turned slightly to the side. It was Greta, one of the art students, the one Denise had mentioned was jealous about Letty's success.

I was so busy twisting back to watch the scene at the lighthouse, my toe hit the edge of the sidewalk. I took several dramatic, faltering steps forward, cupcake tray and all. It seemed my clumsy show had grabbed everyone's attention. They were happy to give me a round of applause when I came out of the near calamity with all cupcakes safe and still wearing their buttercream helmets.

Lola congratulated me on the save as I reached the table. "Well done, and I only briefly had my hand on my phone ready to snap the picture if you went facedown in the cupcakes."

"Gee thanks, buddy."

"Hey, that kind of stuff is Instagram gold."

"Okay, fill me in. What's going on over there?"

"Over where?" Lola straightened up a row of rustic, old cow bells she had brought down to the sale. They clanged as she arranged them in size.

"Seriously? You really don't make note of anything unless you're in the center of it, do you?" I took hold of her shoulders and turned her gently around toward the lighthouse. "The police activity? Officer Chinmoor's patrol car with the glaring red light spinning on top?"

Lola turned back to her bell arrangement. "Please. Chinmoor turns on his alarm when a group of seagulls has landed on the picnic tables."

"But Briggs is there too." Briggs had out his adorable, nifty notepad, his nod to a less techie time. He was talking to a man who looked to be in his thirties. The top half of his long dark hair was pulled back and knotted into a man bun. The unusual hairdo made him easy to recognize as one of the people I saw painting the lighthouse. "It looks like he's talking to the people from the art class."

Lola glanced back briefly to assure me she was highly disinterested in the topic. She pulled a green pillbox hat with a black bow out from under the table. "Look what I found hidden amongst Fiona's treasures. Isn't it adorable?" She pulled off the black cap she was wearing and pushed the green hat down onto her red curls. "And green is the best color for my hair."

"It's very Jackie O. I'm surprised you allowed yourself to shop at the enemy's table."

Fiona was busy rearranging the last few items she had left. It seemed she was spreading them out to make her leftover inventory look more impressive than it actually was.

Lola took off the pillbox hat. "I think the ice cream coma last night helped me reach a moment of zen in my life. I'm not going to fret about little things anymore. Besides, I had to swallow my pride when I saw this amazing hat."

"I guess we all have our breaking points. I've got two more trays in the car."

Lola's footsteps plodded behind me. "I'll grab the second one. It's slow this morning. I think everyone knows the good stuff was bought up yesterday. I've told Mayor Price many times that the flea market should only be for one day."

I heard Lola rattling on about the flea market, but my focus was on the activity across the street. Briggs' face flashed my direction, and we had one of those moments where it seemed our gazes had both been caught up in the same magnetic field. He stared at me a few seconds before nodding politely. I nodded back.

I handed Lola a tray and pulled out the second one.

"You should go over and ask your boyfriend what's happening."

"My boyfriend? You're being especially annoying this morning." We trekked across the grass and pathway to the cupcake table.

Lola picked up one of the lemon cupcakes. "My tip for helping. And you, my opinionated friend, are quick to give me advice about men. But you put up a big brick wall if I try to shower any man wisdom your way."

"That's the problem. It's hardly wisdom." Before she could answer with her acerbic wit, I answered for her and with a good dose of contrition. "No, you're absolutely right, Lola. I'm always sticking my million dollar nose into your business, and you have every right to point out my hypocrisy on the matter."

A short laugh shot from her mouth. "So you admit that Detective Briggs is your boyfriend?"

"Now you're just being crazy."

"I'll take that as a denial with yes undertones." Lola stepped back behind her table.

I stared back at the scene by the lighthouse.

"Oh, for heaven's sake," Lola said sharply. "Go find out what's happening. I can watch the cupcake table."

"Are you sure?"

"Yes. And say hello to your boyfriend," she fired at my back as I hurried off.

Officer Chinmoor and several uniformed officers from Mayfield seemed to be searching for something on the marina and pier. Briggs had just finished up with the man from the art group. He was going through his notes as I walked up behind him.

"Lose something?" I asked. "Or are you guys out on a scavenger hunt?"

Briggs turned to me and a hint of a smile appeared. When he was on duty, he kept them to a minimum, but he always managed a quick, tilted one for me. "Miss Pinkerton, good morning."

I was also always Miss Pinkerton when he was on official business.

"Why are the officers looking in empty boats and behind kiosks?"

"One of the members of the art class is missing. Her car is the blue sedan on the west side of the town square. The group showed up this morning and noticed her car was here, but she was nowhere to be seen. Her phone goes right to voicemail." He looked at his notes. "Scarlet Clark, but she goes by Letty. No one has seen her since last night around midnight after everyone had dinner at Franki's. They had been out here painting the stormy coast. They headed into the diner around ten and stayed there talking and eating until close to midnight."

"Are you suspecting foul play?"

"Not yet. It's too early for that. Hilda is busy contacting the list of family and friends her classmates were able to pull together. She'll probably show up with one of them. It's entirely possible she was having car trouble and called someone to pick her up."

"I'm sure you're right. Well, if you're in the mood for a red velvet cupcake, I'm the cupcake lady this morning."

"Elsie's still off her feet?"

"For another day, I think. Although, I mistakenly gave her a glass of wine after a pain pill last night, and I was pretty sure she thought she could avoid any pain by just flying around town on her wings."

He laughed quietly. "I've heard that combination can give you wings."

"Well, it was nice seeing you. I almost didn't recognize you without your four-footed sidekick."

"Yeah, Conan the Barbarian is back at the office, no doubt causing damage and driving Hilda crazy."

I laughed and pointed to my nose. "Let me know if you need Samantha for anything to help you sniff out the missing person." I'd been jokingly trying to come up with a separate name for my sleuthing nose. Briggs had decided on Samantha, a tribute to the vintage Bewitched television series. Apparently I twitched my nose a lot like the television witch.

"You and Samantha will be the first helpers I call."

CHAPTER 13

*S*unday had definitely been a much slower day at the flea market. Even with the thinner foot traffic, I'd sold half of the cupcakes in an hour. Lola had been busy for ten minutes in a text conversation. Her finger flew over the screen quickly, and with each send, her lips grew tighter with anger. I could only surmise that she was talking to Chuck and hopefully letting him know that they were finished for good. She glanced up in between texts and caught me watching her.

The tight set of her mouth loosened some. "Yes, it's Chuck and yes, I'm telling him to lose my number for good."

"I'm happy to hear it." The flash of Lester's bright blue and red Hawaiian shirt caught my eye. He was walking toward us with two large coffees.

"Yay, the caffeine patrol is here," I sang. "I've got a girls' night hangover."

"Too much wine?" Lester asked as he reached the table.

I took the hot cup of coffee from his hand. "Actually, too much ice cream." I raised the cup to him and to Lola, who was greedily grabbing for her own cup. "Here's to caffeine and friends bearing hot beverages."

I took a sip. "Hmm, comfort food has nothing on a richly brewed cup of coffee. Especially a Lester coffee. How is Elsie doing?"

Lester lifted his sunglasses away from his blue-gray eyes. They had permanent smile lines around them, which fit him well. "She's been ordering me around all morning, so I guess she's almost back to her old self. She tucked herself onto the couch with her heating pad and her down quilt and her television remote that she used like a pointer." He lifted his hand holding an invisible remote and raised his voice to sound like Elsie's. "Les, pull that laundry out of the dryer. Les, see if the plants on the porch need water." He pointed his invisible remote in a different direction and made his voice even squeakier, which was sort of funny since Elsie's voice was about as deep as her brother's. "Les, don't forget to fix that leaky faucet in the bathroom. You've been promising to do it for weeks, and if you don't do it, I'm going to start sending you my water bill. Then you can pay for that leak you refuse to fix."

I took another drink of coffee. "I'd say she's pretty close to a hundred percent then."

"I sure hope so." Lester pulled his glasses back down out of his snow white hair. "She's a pain in the rear when she's well, but she's worse when she's sick."

A tow truck rumbled past on Pickford Way and stopped in front of Letty's parked car. After an hour of activity down at the lighthouse, Detective Briggs and his team had split up and headed different directions. Now it seemed he was back.

Briggs pulled his car up behind the tow truck. The burly truck driver climbed out, his sleeves rolled to his elbows and his forearms covered with tattoos. He was carrying the long, thin hooked device tow truck drivers used to unlock your car when you left your keys inside.

"I heard something about a missing woman," Lester said as we all turned to watch the driver shimmy the thin piece of metal between the top of the window and the thick rubber seal.

"Yes, one of the art students who came to town to paint the lighthouse disappeared last night. Her friends can't seem to locate her," I said. "That's her car. It's been parked there all night."

"An artist? Then she's probably just flitting around town with friends," Lester said with a dry laugh. "You know how flighty those artists can be."

I looked over at him with raised brows.

"Sorry," he grumbled. "It seems after following a night of unlucky poker playing with a morning of being ordered about by Queen Elsie and her royal remote scepter, I've grown cranky. I'm sure the woman will show up." His focus turned back to the car. "Looks like they've already got the car open."

Detective Briggs disappeared inside the car and spent a good amount of time searching between and under seats. While he worked, the tow truck driver used a crow bar to pop open the trunk.

"Maybe Briggs could use that super nose of yours to look for clues," Lester suggested.

"Yes but I've still got a few dozen cupcakes to sell."

"Minus one." Lester picked up a red velvet and unwrapped it. "I earned this. Go on, now. I'll look after the table. I'd much rather be out here with the baked goods than with the actual baker."

I glanced over at Lola. She waved me on. "Go ahead. Lester and I can handle things here."

"Thanks so much, guys." I headed over to Letty's car and poked my head into the open door.

Briggs was twisted and turned into an impressive yoga stretch as he reached for something under the back of the passenger seat. He emerged victoriously with a tube of yellow paint.

He looked up in surprise. "Lacey," he cleared his throat, "Miss Pinkerton, I didn't see you there."

"Didn't mean to sneak up on you. Any luck finding the missing woman?"

Briggs climbed out of the front seat holding the tube of paint and an empty coffee mug. "No, and it seems her car isn't going to lend any assistance. She keeps it pretty neat. I was hoping to find her phone."

Briggs walked around to look into the empty trunk. He rummaged through a few shopping totes and a box of paints and brushes. "Thanks, Frank," he said to the tow truck driver. "I'll give you a call if we need to have the vehicle towed."

"Sure thing, Detective Briggs." The driver nodded at me and headed back to his truck.

Briggs pulled out his notebook and leaned against the car. "I'm afraid we've received some information that made this missing person case more urgent. Ms. Dean, the art teacher, said she and Letty and the rest of the class were heading back to their cars. She noticed that Letty stopped to answer a call. She strolled along the sidewalk finishing her conversation. Ms. Dean and the others climbed in their cars and drove away. Ms. Dean never saw her finish the conversation or climb into her car. While we were trying to track down Letty's parents, they were traveling through Europe, Hilda received a frantic call from Letty's mom. She was calling from some village in Italy, and therefore had a very hard time getting the connection through to Port Danby. She claimed that she had called Letty around midnight, our time, and that five minutes into the call Letty gasped and the phone call was abruptly lost. She tried to get a connection again but failed. She insisted that she heard a shocked gasp before the call ended."

"That doesn't sound good. But with a weak, international signal, maybe she misheard the sound."

"Let's hope that's the case. Officer Chinmoor has been out to

Letty's place. She lives alone in a rental house in Chesterton. There was no sign of her or of any disturbance at the house. I'm going there right now to look around."

I stood up straighter. "Can I come? I could take a whiff of some of her things, perfume, shampoo and get a sense of the fragrances she might use. I don't know if it'll help."

"Actually, that's a great idea. I sent word to the state police that I might need the search dogs soon." He stopped and looked mortified by what he'd just said. "Not that I think of you like a search dog."

I sputtered a laugh. "It's all right, Detective Briggs. I don't mind. Just don't expect me to crawl around this marina on all fours sniffing the ground."

"Never."

CHAPTER 14

$\mathcal{L}$etty Clark's house was at the end of a quiet cul-de-sac that was dotted with small cottage like houses. A few of the yards were well kept with flowers and nicely trimmed front lawns and a few, Letty's included, were unkempt, with lawns that were more weeds than grass and flower boxes that looked as if they hadn't seen a bloom in years. Letty's house looked particularly neglected with peeling paint, dangling shutters and splotchy roof shingles.

"When we were interviewing the other artists, one of the women, Denise, told us that Letty kept a key hidden in the usual place, under a potted plant on the porch." He tilted his head toward me. "A terrible idea, by the way. It's the first place thieves look."

"I will keep that in mind."

There was only one pot on the porch. It was filled with soil but the plant was only a few tattered stems. I concluded that it had at one time been a potted fern.

Briggs lifted the pot and pulled out the key. He opened the front door and we walked inside. My nose was instantly assaulted by the smell of oil paints and thinner. It was strong enough to make my eyes water. I fanned my face to dry them.

"That paint smell is strong for me," Briggs said. "I can only imagine how overwhelming it is for you."

"Very. She needs to open some windows. It can't be good for her either." I spoke of the woman in present tense in full hopes that she was alive and well somewhere hanging out with friends.

Detective Briggs went straight to a tiny desk in the corner of the kitchen. There were a few notes and an address book sitting on what seemed to be this week's grocery list. I headed down a short hallway to a bathroom that was so small you could wash your hands from the toilet, although that would be rather counterproductive. Still, if one was in a pinch for time . . .

The dated pink ceramic tile vanity top was cluttered with cosmetics, hair products and moisturizing lotions. My job at the flower shop required me to slather up my hands, morning and night. I imagined it would be the same for someone who spent a lot of time with oil paints and the harsh chemicals needed to clean brushes.

A bottle of perfume sitting next to a hairbrush smelled distinctly of bergamot, a fresh citrus scent that was very popular in the perfume industry. I felt a little uneasy about going through her cosmetics and personal products, but I sniffed each one, trying to memorize every scent. It was possible one of the smells would come in handy in finding Letty.

I walked back out to the front room. Detective Briggs opened a door that led off the front room, adjacent to the kitchen. As he swung it open, I swayed on my feet, lightheaded from the pungent chemical scent that flowed out of the room.

"Are you all right?" Briggs asked.

"Yes. Just wasn't expecting that toxic cloud."

He looked into the room. "It seems we've found the source of the paint smell."

The odor was dizzying, but I was drawn into the room by the incredible art work placed haphazardly around the space, leaning on old furniture, against the walls and even on the window sill. In the center of the room, Letty had stretched out a painter's tarp with an easel sitting at just the right angle to catch the daylight coming through the window. The front tray of the easel was cluttered with crumpled tubes of paint, rolled from the back ends like tubes of toothpaste being pressured to give up their last squirt of paste. The half painted canvas on the easel was a glorious collection of lavender blooming jacarandas being replicated from a postcard that was push pinned to the top of the easel.

"She's truly talented." My voice floated around the fume-filled room. Suddenly a cold, eerie feeling swept through me.

Briggs seemed to notice. "What's wrong? Is it the chemical odors? Too much?" He fired out the questions in that worried tone that always warmed me. This time it was a little more subdued than a few months back when he'd discovered I'd gone on a plane ride with Dash along the coastline. He was frantic with concern about it, so much so that he had angrily lectured me about the risk just before admitting he had been worried about me. I'd tucked the moment in my heart but also cautioned myself not to overthink it.

"It's not the noxious fumes, although they are making me feel as if my head might just lift off my neck and drift away. I just felt a chill of sorts." I looked at him. "Briggs, tell me what is your gut instinct on this missing person case?"

Briggs looked around the room, seemingly to avoid direct eye contact with me. That reaction said it all.

"You think something bad has happened to Letty?" I asked, already knowing the answer.

"It doesn't look good." Briggs stared down at a painting that was near his foot. It was a portrait, a familiar face. We both recognized it at the same time.

Briggs lifted the painting to hold it up to the light. "Darren Morgan," he said to himself.

"He's with the art group, right? I saw you talking to him yesterday." Morgan was the young man with the long hair and man bun. He had striking features, but the artist's hand had muted some of the harsh expression in his face as if he was someone she admired or even loved.

"Yes, he mentioned that he and Letty were friends. He seemed appropriately concerned about her, at least for an acquaintance or friend." He surveyed the painting a minute longer before putting it back in its spot.

"When I look at that painting, I see the caring, loving strokes of an artist and the face of a model who were more than friends. But that is just a mere observation by someone who doesn't know much about art."

Briggs rubbed the stubble on his jaw with his forefinger and thumb as he looked at the painting again. "I don't know much about art either, but I'd say you might be right about that. I may have to talk to Morgan again." We headed out of the room and he shut the door.

"I've got a tentative catalog of scents in my head from the items in the bathroom. Don't know if they'll come in handy though."

We walked down the short hallway past the bathroom. Briggs opened the only other door. It led to a small bedroom and bed that was covered with a pink plaid quilt. A few stuffed teddy bears sat against the pillow, scowling at us as if telling us we had no right to be in the room. A sweater was hanging on a chair near the window.

"I'm going to need something for the tracking dogs to use for scent." As he picked up the sweater, I noticed the painting and the Victorian dressed doll from Fiona Diggle's table were sitting on top of the dresser. I walked over to it and fingered the doll's lacy dress. The head had been turned at a grotesque angle so that the pretty porcelain face was nearly facing back over the doll's shoulder. "Letty bought these at the flea market. She thought this painting might be valuable, but your former art teacher, Ms. Dean, laughed at the notion. Later that day, Jodie came back looking for the painting, but Letty had purchased it."

A blue and silver business card for an auction house was sitting between the doll and the painting. I picked it up. "Let us sell your valued treasures for top dollar," I read from the card.

Briggs joined me at the dresser. "Maybe the painting was valuable after all." He squinted at the signature that was mostly camouflaged by the sea of dark green and purple mountain lupines spread out from the forefront of the painting. "I can't read that signature, can you?"

I tiptoed and got a closer look. It was just a swirl of black paint. "I think the first letter of the last name might be G, but it could also be an S. So I guess that is no help at all. I know I shouldn't be touching this, but I feel bad for this doll. Her face is twisted back so far it reminds me of that movie, *The Exorcist*." I reached up and gently turned the head, much to my surprise *and* horror, the head came off in my hand. "Oops. Didn't realize it would be so delicate."

Briggs pressed his knuckles against his mouth to stifle a laugh as I quickly pushed the head back onto the body. I held my hand underneath for a second to make sure it was secure and then stepped back. "Last time I'll feel sorry for a doll."

Briggs' phone rang as we walked out of the bedroom. "Briggs here." I followed him out of the house and locked the door for him as he finished his conversation.

I pushed the key under the plant in case Letty returned home and had lost her own keys.

"That was the K-9 search team. They're on their way to Port Danby right now. Let's head back."

CHAPTER 15

I stood near the lighthouse and back from the official business and watched with no small amount of admiration as Detective Briggs stepped into his role as lead officer, instructing his people on the next steps in the search. Two black Labradors and a tall, sharp-eared German Shepherd waited impatiently at the ends of their tethers, anxious to get their noses to the ground. Intermittent barks filled the air, garnering even more attention from curious onlookers in the area. Officer Chinmoor was put in charge of keeping spectators out of the area, but he was having a hard time of it. It seemed the second he shored up the dam in one location, another hole opened up, allowing spectators to leak through. Briggs noticed that Chinmoor was struggling. He strode over to the people gathered on the sidewalk, pushing and scooting closer to the police activity. A few curt commands and a well-perfected detective glower caused the entire group to disperse and walk dejectedly back toward the town square.

I glanced back toward the town square. Lola was still not at her table. I'd gone straight over to the flea market after Briggs and I had gotten back to Port Danby. Having sold all the cupcakes, Lester had already packed up for the day. Lola had left a sign that she was closed for lunch.

Briggs and one of the canine officers broke off from the group and walked to the rarely used trailhead that led down toward the rocky coastline below Pickford Lighthouse. The surge from the brief but turbulent rainstorm had receded leaving behind gobs of tangled seaweed and bits of debris on the ridge of rocks that acted as a natural wall between the erosive ocean tide and the cliff side beneath the Pickford Lighthouse. The only way down to the rocks was a steep, precarious trail that was dotted with warning signs to keep off the rocks and beware of high tide. A short chain link fence had been erected at the top of the trail with yet another warning sign that the trail and rocks were dangerous. It was a somewhat comically inadequate deterrent for people who might be feeling adventurous or suicidal or stupid. Or a combination of all three. Briggs and the officer, a small, athletic looking woman with short black hair seemed to be contemplating a search down at the rocks. I didn't envy anyone having to travel that steep, narrow path or the treacherous outcropping of granite and shale.

A cluster of cottony clouds slipped away from the sun. Light and heat poured down on the ocean below as I stared out to the horizon. It was turning out to be an unseasonably warm day, especially after a night of wind and rain. The cold, harsh night of weather made it seem even less likely that Letty had stayed out voluntarily. The icy feeling of dread that had overtaken me when I stood in her art room had stayed with me long after Briggs and I left the house.

It seemed the strategy planning session was over. The dogs headed off in three different directions. Briggs headed toward me.

"It seems you've got noses that are far superior to mine working for you now," I noted lightly as he reached me.

"I don't know if they're far superior, but they don't mind hiking down treacherous paths or through thickets of overgrown brush. They've got a lot to cover. They'll start here at the marina and lighthouse, then head to some of the wilderness areas around Mayfield and the rural areas off Highway 48. We don't have much to go on to pinpoint a location, but we know she was last seen here."

"Those dogs are so well trained," I said as we watched them nose to ground, lead their human partners on the search.

"Yeah," Briggs said wryly. "That's what a trained dog looks like. Actually, the shepherd reminds me of the dog I grew up with. I named him Yogi. When I was twelve, my mom decided I was old enough to be on my own afterschool, so she went back to work."

"Yogi? I love that name."

It was rare for Briggs to talk about his past or his childhood. I leaned closer, not wanting to miss a word. I was fascinated to hear about a twelve-year-old James Briggs.

"Yes, naming him after a picnic basket stealing cartoon bear was probably a little beneath the dog. Yogi had tall pointed black ears like the search dog. He would sit at the front door like a security guard when my parents were out. When I came home from school, he greeted me with licks and barks and then he set to work being my protector. It was kind of nice. I never would have confessed to my parents that I was kind of scared being on my own in the house but because of Yogi, I got past that easily. He was my only family for three hours after school and I loved that dog. I think that's why I never got another one. Yogi was irreplaceable."

His story made my throat tighten up. I wasn't used to seeing that vulnerable side of Briggs. I liked it.

The side door to the lighthouse opened, and Marty Tate walked out with a broom. It was a warm spring day but he was still bundled in a scarf and sweater. He shuffled his feet as he moved a straw broom in slow strokes across the cement path around the lighthouse.

Briggs and I walked over to say hello.

Marty's milky eyes peered up over the folds of his scarf. His gnarled fingers reached up to pull the knitted wool down from his mouth. "They still haven't found that poor girl? That's a shame." He clucked his tongue exactly like my grandmother used to do when I spilled milk on the counter or got caught sneaking a cookie.

"I'm afraid the team will be trespassing here for the rest of the afternoon, Marty," Briggs said.

"No problem, I'm just doing a few chores. I opened the light-house up for a few hours yesterday, and people tracked in all kinds of grass and dirt."

I stared up at the tall tower and swayed on my feet with a flash of vertigo. "That's right, I was going to try and get over for the tour. I'm sorry I missed it. I've been dying to see what the view is like from the lantern room."

Marty inclined his head toward the open doorway. "You can take a quick look right now, before I head back to the house for lunch."

"If you're sure you don't mind," I said already making my way to the door.

"Just mind those stairs. They are quite a climb," Marty warned.

I stepped into the base of the lighthouse. The structure of white stucco and brick shot up like a tube with the only light coming from the lantern house and the sporadic small windows cut out of the thick walls. The first set of steps were brick risers topped with worn oak. They were short and squat like the steps leading up to a front porch on a house. But beyond the squat set of stairs were the black metal steps that led straight up to the top in a steep coiled pattern. It reminded me of the death defying tracks of a roller coaster.

I was feeling slightly callous for treating myself to a quick light-house tour while there was a team of people searching for a missing woman right outside the walls, but since my nasal services were no longer needed I had a few spare minutes.

An eerie whistling sound pierced through the edge of the door and circled up to the top of the tower like the howling winds on an autumn night. The sound grew dimmer and seemed to fade away completely once it reached the capped ceiling, but then another gust seeped in and started the cycle again. It was like the constant roar of the ocean, nature's never-ending music.

It was definitely colder inside the lighthouse than outside in the warm spring sun. I zipped up my sweatshirt and climbed the squat low steps leading to the black curlicue of metal stairs. As I passed a door, painted a sickly green like the color you might see on the walls of a hospital, I caught a whiff of a rancid, unpleasant odor. A tarnished metal lock was looped through a latch on the door. I moved closer and scrunched up my nose to keep the taste of the smell out of my throat. It was a smell that was as rare as it was easy to recognize. It was the pungent, nauseating smell of death. It seemed that something flesh and bone was decomposing behind the hospital green door.

Adrenaline was pumping through all cylinders as I raced quickly down the steps and out into the fresh air. I urgently scanned the area and found the broad-shouldered figure I was looking for. He was checking off an area on the map they'd created for the search.

I raced across the lawn. "Briggs," I called and stopped for a breath when I reached him. "I need you to come with me. Something's not right in the lighthouse."

Briggs folded the map up and pushed it under his arm. We race walked back to the lighthouse. Marty was on the opposite side still sweeping the pathway at a painstakingly slow pace.

"There's a locked door on the bottom tier of the lighthouse. The strong odor of decay is seeping beneath the thin space under that door," I uttered between breaths.

"Like something is dead inside?" he asked.

"Yes."

"Let's see if Marty has a key with him."

Marty looked up, surprised to see us approach so quickly. He stopped and rested on the broom, using it like a walking stick. "Where's the fire?" he asked with a gritty laugh.

"No fire," Briggs assured him. "There's a locked door on the bottom floor of the lighthouse."

Marty's frizzled gray brows inched up like caterpillars.

"It's painted in a pale green color and has a tarnished lock looped through the latch," I clarified.

His caterpillar brows relaxed. "Yeah, of course. The storage closet. Nothing much in there but a few boxes of manuals. Instructions on running the lantern in fog and whatnot."

"I need to get a look inside that storage closet, if you don't mind, Marty." Briggs started moving in the direction of the door. He was getting slightly impatient with Marty's sluggish, ninety-something manner.

"No problem. Go right ahead." Marty stayed frozen to the spot hanging onto his broom like Father Time holding onto his long sickle.

Briggs erased the four sharp steps forward he'd taken and returned to Marty. "Do you have the key to the lock?"

"Key?" Marty repeated.

I rested my hand on Marty's arm to get his attention. He turned his milky gaze my direction. "Marty, there's a lock on that door, and we'd like to see what's inside it."

"Yes, go right ahead," he said again.

I noticed the tiny twitch in Briggs' cheek that signaled his patience was wearing thin.

"Could you give us the key?" I asked politely.

"Key?" Marty repeated again.

This time my bracing hand landed on Briggs.

"You don't need any key," Marty continued. "That lock has been broken for years."

Briggs was halfway to the lighthouse door before Marty got the final syllable out. He dashed inside. I caught up to him as he was yanking open the broken lock. He pushed the back of his hand against his nose to block the smell. I stood back a few feet, not anxious to see what was behind the door.

Briggs disappeared inside. "Yuck." It wasn't exactly the professional response I was expecting from a detective discovering a dead body. His face appeared around the door. "It's not the missing woman. It's a dead squirrel. It must have slipped inside the closet when Marty wasn't looking and got locked in."

A burst of air blew from my lips in relief. "Thank goodness." A whistling sound filled the mostly hollow tower again. Briggs stepped briskly out of the closet.

"That's just the wind," I assured him.

The whistle blew again but louder and more urgently. Briggs slammed shut the closet door. "That's not the wind. That's the search team letting us know they've found something."

He raced out of the lighthouse. I followed quickly behind.

CHAPTER 16

A wave of nausea passed through me as the lifeless lump was brought up from beneath the clutter of seaweed on the rocks. I'd spent some years in medical school, until making the tough decision to quit. During those years I'd had plenty of opportunities to view, examine and even dissect dead bodies. I'd also seen more than one murder victim up close while lending Detective Briggs my nose and sleuthing skills. But seeing Letty's lifeless form being pulled from the jagged rocks and ocean debris was hard to watch.

Her salt-water soaked, rubbery body bounced and tossed back and forth on the gurney during the difficult trek back up the trail. Several times, the officers had to stop and reposition their feet and their holds on the stretcher to avoid sliding down, victim and all, to the rocks below. Each time, a collective breath was held by those of us who waited at the head of the trail.

Officer Chinmoor had finally managed crowd control, and all spectators had been moved back to the flea market across the street. Two of the people from the art class, Jodie and Denise, had spent the morning at the town square waiting for word about Letty, but I no longer saw their faces in the crowd. Mayor Price had come out of his office at least three times to get an update but didn't seem to have the stomach for watching a dead body come up from the rocks. He had walked off rather hurriedly, and we hadn't seen him since.

The search crew circled around the victim, making a human and canine curtain of sorts, while Detective Briggs examined the body. I drew in a breath of refreshing coastal air to quiet the nausea before edging my way into the circle. No one seemed to question my presence. Briggs had made it clear I was there with him for investigative reasons.

Letty's naturally pale skin had taken on a gray-blue sheen and sand dripped from the sides of her ashen lips. A strand of seaweed was wrapped around her body somewhat like a sash in a beauty pageant. Briggs pulled out a pocket knife and cut the tubular plant away from Letty's chest.

I covered a gasp, not wanting to seem like a complete amateur in a circle of professionals. "Looks like we just found the cause of death, and it had nothing to do with the storm surge or that treacherous trail," Briggs said as he peeled back some of the ripped fabric of Letty's black sweater. The dark color of the sweater and the hours spent soaking in the ocean had washed away a lot of the blood, but the gash just below her throat looked lethal.

"A knife wound, from the looks of it." Briggs reached for his notepad. He stood up and looked back down the difficult trail. "It's hard to believe the murderer would have gone through the trouble of carrying the body down there to dispose of it. It just took three of you to bring the body up to the top. I'm thinking the murder happened somewhere up the beach. The tide moves west from the marina to Pickford Beach before heading this direction below the lighthouse." Briggs wrote something down on his notes.

"The coroner is here," one of the officers said.

Nate Blankenship, the local coroner, drove up onto the lighthouse lawn and parked strategically to block any view of the scene
from the town square.

I walked over to where Briggs was standing. "It seems my nose
is not going to help with this case."

My statement seemed to remind him that he had a search crew
waiting for further instructions. "Team, thanks for your help
today. I know you've got a drive ahead of you and your dogs will
be tired and hungry and ready to head home. Good work."

The officers and their dogs headed back to the their vehicles.
Nate Blankenship set to work with a visual inspection of the body.

Briggs was still trying to figure out the murder path. His gaze
circled the area, including where Letty's car was parked. "I think
the murderer stabbed Miss Clark somewhere near the beach and
then pushed her body into the water thinking it would be taken
out to sea."

"But last night's storm surge would have pushed her right back
to shore." I looked back toward the lighthouse. "And the natural
flow of the tide brought her to the rocks below the lighthouse."

"It would explain why we didn't find the body in our prelimi-
nary search," Briggs added.

I stepped forward and landed on something rubbery. I gasped
and stumbled back, worried that I'd stepped on the victim.

"It's just the seaweed." Briggs lifted it up.

"Wait just a second," I said quickly before he tossed it aside. He
held it up for me to examine. Seaweed was like no other plant in
the world, with its plastic looking leaves, hollow tubular stems and
bulb shaped protrusions. Which was why it was exceptionally easy
to spot the branch of laurel jammed between the thick leaves. I
pulled the stem free from the seaweed. Several black threads hung
from the sharp broken edge of the branch.

Briggs moved in closer. "I'd say those are threads from the

victim's sweater. That plant doesn't look like anything from the sea."

"No, it's not. It's laurel, like the hedge that runs along the western edge of Pickford Beach."

"Let's head over there. Hey, Nate, I'll be right back."

The coroner who was crouched down over the body waved back over his shoulder.

We headed along the walking path that stretched between the lighthouse and the section of pavement that led down to the westernmost side of Pickford Beach. The laurel hedge started at the end of the pavement and bordered a walkway that circled the far end of the beach. The dense, waxy shrub created a small cove.

Briggs stopped and examined the hedge. "I don't see any place where a body might have been dragged through to get to the water. The wind and rain would have washed away a trail if something had been dragged across the sand."

The hedge ended about fifteen feet from where the water lapped at the shore. It was a gentle tide, but the night before the shoreline would have looked much different.

"See that ridge of debris?" I pointed to the line of wood splinters, shells and bits of seaweed that stretched along the sand. "That ridge shows how far up the storm surge came. It came up right up to the laurel hedge."

I turned back to the thick shrubby border. As I moved, something shiny caught my eye. I knelt down in front of the laurel and poked my arm through to the cell phone that was jammed between the branches. I pulled it free and pinched it between two fingers, not wanting to disturb any prints that might be left on it.

Briggs reached into his pocket and pulled out a glove and evidence bag. "The rain probably washed away any prints, but I'll bet anything this phone belongs to the victim." He put on the glove and examined it. The case and glass were scratched. He pushed the button on top and shook his head. "Either it was ruined in the rain or the battery needs charging." He dropped it into the baggie. "Good work, Miss Pinkerton. After a thorough search for evidence, I need to go back and interview the people from the art class. Starting with the man in the portrait, Darren Morgan."

CHAPTER 17

a murder had put a damper on the day. Several of the flea market vendors had packed up and cleared out, leaving the occasional empty table between the sellers determined to squeeze every last dollar out of the remaining shoppers. Lola was more than happy to shut down for the day. I helped her pile the last unsold items into her car, and we headed back to the antique shop.

"I can't believe that quiet little artist was murdered," Lola said as she turned the car onto Harbor Lane. "Can't imagine she'd have many enemies." Just as she finished the statement, Lester's pub tables came into view. The Coffee Hutch wasn't open, but Ryder was perched on a stool. Denise was sitting across from him, huddled in a white sweater and holding a tissue.

Lola made a puffy sound. "Boy, someone went straight for the sympathy card."

"Lola," I said with some degree of scold, "we can assume Denise and Letty knew each other pretty well if they were in art class together. I'm sure Ryder is just lending a supportive ear."

Properly chastised and possibly feeling a little guilty about her previous statement, Lola fell unusually silent. I caught Ryder's gaze a few times as he watched us pull up to the antique store in Lola's car. She sat still, staring straight ahead, her black cap pulled down tightly around her red curls.

"I've got the afternoon free," I said quietly. "I could help you carry the stuff back into the store."

Lola shook her head. "No, thanks. I'm tired. I think I'll just leave the things in the car until tomorrow."

"If you're sure." My car was parked on the other side of the street. I opened the passenger door and stuck out a foot. "You know he likes you a lot, Lola. If you'd just put down your guard for a second, you'd see it."

She nodded without looking at me. "Speaking of letting down your guard, how was your day with Detective Briggs?"

"Touché, my friend. And well deserved. See you tomorrow." I climbed out of the car and walked across the street.

Ryder waved me over to the table. I was rather anxious to talk to Denise anyhow. I was hoping to get a little more insight into the various relationships between the members of the art class.

I reached the table. Denise provided me with a sad, teary eyed frown, but that vanished quickly with her first question. "I saw you at the lighthouse when they brought Letty's body out of the water. How could you stand to watch?" She dotted her eyes with the tissue but tears didn't really go with her enthusiasm to find out how I'd stomached the murder scene.

Ryder saw that I was slightly stunned by her question and kindly responded for me. "Lacey went to medical school, and she assists in some of the murder investigations."

Denise's dark brown eyes were round as saucers. "You do? A flower shop owner? I don't understand."

Ryder was about to jump in again, but I decided to shut down the inquiry into my life. I had an inquiry of my own. "You must be terribly upset about Letty's death. Were you two very close?"

"We were good friends." Denise tried the tissue routine once more, but even she seemed to realize she was pushing it. She crumpled up the tissue in her fist. "Of course, Letty was much older. Like six or seven years," she added to qualify what she deemed as much older. "Not old enough to die of course."

"Of course." I shot a secret wink at Ryder. "Denise, do you have any idea who might want to hurt Letty?"

Denise put her hand against her chest in shock, and I realized, too late, she didn't realize it was murder. "You mean she didn't just fall accidentally into the water? That's what Jodie and I concluded. How awful that someone might have killed her."

"Oh, no, there's no way of knowing yet how she died," I lied. The horrid gash in Letty's chest left no doubt it was murder, but I might have opened my mouth too soon.

"Right, I'm sure the police still have a lot of investigation to do," Ryder added to help out with my misstep.

"Poor Letty," Denise sighed. "She had a great career ahead of her. She was so talented." She stretched out the word *so*. "In fact, she was doing so well—" She sat up straighter. "Now that you mention it, Greta Bailey from class sure didn't have a great affection for Letty. She was monstrously jealous. Greta has been working so hard to get noticed in the art world. She even had a few art galleries and collectors interested in her work, but then Letty's paintings came along and took the shine right off of Greta. Everything fell through for her after that. I wouldn't be surprised if Greta was jealous enough to do something awful to Letty."

"No, Denise, we can't go making up murder scenarios," I said quickly to stop her theorizing.

"Besides," Ryder interjected, "doesn't an artist's death just make their artwork more desirable? Killing her competitor would not help Greta in the long run."

Denise looked at Ryder the same way Nevermore stared up at me while I was opening his cat food, with admiration, longing and a touch of good old-fashioned lust. Ryder was going to have to cut this friendship short if he didn't want to give Denise the wrong impression.

"Of course, there's also the torrid on-again, off-again relationship Letty was having with Darren. He's the guy with the long hair and man bun."

"Yes, I've seen him." As much as I didn't want Denise to go off on an uninformed spree of murder theories, I was interested in Darren's relationship with Letty."

"So Letty and Darren dated?"

"If that's what you call it." She rolled her eyes. "One minute they were playing kissy face and the next cold shoulder. Like two teenagers, seriously. I can't believe the way thirty-somethings play games with each other."

"Yes, we millennials certainly have social relationships down to a texting, twittering art," I said wryly.

Ryder stifled a laugh, but Denise didn't seem to catch on to the sarcasm.

"All I know is that I was certain Darren took the class just to be closer to Letty. He's an all right artist, but he's not very into the class. And once Letty's career started taking off, she had even less time and interest in Darren. I'll just bet he was so heartbroken about it all, he killed her," she pronounced with a dramatic, confident flare.

"Again, Denise, it's not a good idea to start accusing people until the facts are uncovered."

Denise's phone buzzed and she glanced at it. "It's a text from Greta. She's acting all shocked and upset. I'll bet it's just an act, you know, to throw the scent off of her. She wants to hang out, but I think I'll avoid her just in case—" She lowered her voice to a whisper. "In case she's a murderer."

Even though I'd gotten a few significant details about the relationships Letty'd had with her art classmates, I wasn't sure it was worth it. Denise seemed to be fully immersed in the world of intrigue, jealousy, heartbreak and murder now.

"Hey, boss," Ryder said suddenly, "didn't we need to go over that paperwork and those numbers about the flower thing for the—" He stuttered, looking for a word.

"The wedding," I supplied. "Why yes, if you have time right now we could work on that."

Denise pouted for a second. "I guess I should head home anyhow. I'll call you later, Ryder."

Ryder and I made our pretend exit to the flower shop. I pulled out my keys and opened the door, and we stepped inside to make it look good.

Denise climbed into her car and drove off. Ryder released an audible sigh.

"You are going to have to cut the cord clean and simple, Ryder. Otherwise, it's going to get harder and harder to saw through it."

"Trust me, I know."

I patted his shoulder. "Guess it's not easy being a nice guy, eh?"

"It's always been my downfall. I noticed Lola drove off fast. I was going to offer to help her with her antiques."

"I think she was tired from the long weekend."

Ryder's bangs hung low over his face but he didn't brush them away like usual. He was thinking about Lola.

"Don't give up on her yet, Ryder. Sometimes Lola makes things more complicated than they are, but she'll come around."

He shrugged as if it didn't matter to him, but I knew it did. "I've got more to worry about anyhow, like prying the Denise barnacle off my hull."

I laughed at the analogy. With the coast clear, we headed back outside.

"So was it murder?" Ryder asked.

"Sure as the million dollar nose on my face." I locked up the shop.

"That's scary. Isn't it true that sometimes the killer tries to implicate motives for other people to lead the police off their trail?"

"I suppose a really diabolical murderer might do that. Why do you ask?"

We walked toward our cars. "No reason really, except Denise sure was going out of her way to solve the murder just now."

"True. Guess you better let her down slow and easy."

Ryder turned a worried look my way.

I laughed. "I'm kidding. I think she was just throwing out ideas because she likes to stay the center of a conversation."

"Hope you're right. See you tomorrow, boss. Then we can go over the paperwork about the thing with the flowers."

"Indeed," I said with a laugh.

CHAPTER 18

*M*y insatiable curiosity stopped me at the end of Harbor Lane where I quickly made a U-turn and headed back toward Pickford Way. I was interested in knowing if Detective Briggs had uncovered any more evidence since I'd left the scene. Even though Denise was doling out wild, unfounded conspiracy theories, I decided it couldn't hurt to let Briggs know what she'd said about Letty's unsteady relationship with Darren Morgan and Greta's jealousy over Letty's success.

I pulled up alongside the town square. About half the vendors seemed to be sticking it out until the prearranged four o'clock closing time. Most probably figured that since they had taken the time and energy to carry the stuff to the flea market, they might as well see it until the end. After all, the more things sold, the less that had to be loaded up and hauled away.

It seemed that Detective Briggs was done for the afternoon. He was at the trunk of his car packing away gloves and bags used for collecting evidence.

"Miss Pinkerton," he said sounding a touch weary but none-theless genuinely pleased to see me.

"You must be tired." I leaned against the side of his car.

"Hungry more than tired. I've got a sandwich at the office. And I need to get back there because Hilda wants to head home. She was watching the puppy for me, making sure he didn't destroy the police station while I was gone."

"How did the evidence search go?"

"Fantastic." He reached into the trunk of the car and pulled out an evidence bag. The bag contained a knife, a knife with a mother-of-pearl inlay on the handle. "The blade has been washed by the rain, but we're hoping to find some traces of blood and prints on it."

I jumped to attention. "I know this knife. At least I think I do." I stretched my neck to get a view of the vendors in the town square. Roger, the chef with the fancy knife set, was still selling his kitchen wares.

Briggs followed my line of sight. "It is a unique knife. Did you see it at the flea market?"

"An entire set of them, actually. That man over there with the handlebar moustache is a retired chef. He was selling a lovely set of knives, each with a mother-of-pearl handle just like this one."

"Excellent. Let's go see if the knives are still there." Briggs slid the evidence bag into his inside pocket. I caught a rare glimpse of his shoulder holster and gun.

We headed across the street. I favored him with a smug grin. "Guess it's a good thing I stopped by."

He glanced sideways at me. "I guess so. To be honest, I hadn't even thought about looking for similar knives at the flea market. I'm going to blame it on lack of sustenance. I just hope the puppy hasn't helped himself to my chicken sandwich."

"I hope, especially since it's chicken, that it's in the staff refrigerator."

"It is but I wouldn't put it past that dog to figure out how to open the fridge. He's very smart."

"Bragged the proud dad," I teased.

"I'm not Dad and I'm not bragging. I'm fretting about my lunch."

The gelled curlicues on the ends of Roger's moustache were wilting into icicles from a long day under the sun. He'd pulled on a cap, but it seemed he'd thought about sun protection a few hours too late. His round cheeks were bright red as he packed some copper measuring spoons into a box.

"I'm just packing up," he said to us without looking up. "Let me know if you have any questions."

"I was wondering about the pearl handled knife set I saw here yesterday," I said.

He looked up from his task and glanced at Detective Briggs before bringing a smile back to me. "Told you that you should have bought that set. I sold it this morning—half price."

"Half price? That's a nice discount."

Roger closed the packing box flaps. "I had no choice. Not sure when it happened, but I guess when I turned my back for a second, someone walked off with one of the carving knives. So the set was incomplete. But the customer was thrilled to have it for that price."

"Roger, this is Detective Briggs. He has a few questions about those knives."

Briggs pulled out his notebook and lifted his coat to show the badge on his belt.

Roger stuck out his hand for a shake. "Of course, Detective Briggs. Thank you for keeping our towns safe. Although, I guess there was a terrible incident across the street at the lighthouse. Did the poor girl fall to her death? Kids are always hanging out near that trail. It's a dangerous place."

"Yes, it is." Briggs reached into his coat pocket. "I wonder if you could tell us whether or not this knife came from the set."

Roger's moustache teeter tottered over his pursed mouth as he squinted through the plastic. He reached into his cash box and pulled out a pair of wire-rimmed glasses. He put them on. Briggs held the knife closer.

Roger's face smoothed with surprise. "Why yes, that's it. That's the missing knife." He seemed to be fitting the pieces together and the surprise turned to concern. "Good lord, did someone steal that knife to kill the poor girl?"

"We'll have to let the coroner and lab techs decide that." Briggs saw that the knife was causing Roger some distress. He returned it to its place inside his coat. "Who purchased the knife set? Just for our records," he added quickly. "In case I need to have the rest of the knife set put into evidence."

"Well, I don't know her name, but I think she was with the group of painters." Roger's brows bunched together. "That girl you found was a painter too, wasn't she? My word, I wonder if there was a connection?"

It appeared that just like Denise, Roger was going to head off into his own mystery solving moment, but Briggs was more effective at stopping accusations and theories.

"There is very likely no connection. Which of the painters was it? Could you describe her?"

Roger tapped his chin, and his moustache twitched as he thought about it. He lifted a thick hand. Briggs readied his pen over his notepad.

"She was about so high and forty something. Not the most pleasant woman in the world, a little brusque, if you ask me."

Briggs stopped writing. "Brusque? Are there any other details, hair color perhaps?"

"Actually, Detective Briggs," I spoke up, "I think I know the person he's talking about."

"Right. Thank you, Mr. Brooking. You've been very helpful."

We left the table and headed back across the street. "The

woman's name is Greta Bailey." We stopped at his car, and Briggs wrote down the name.

"I don't want to keep you from your late, late lunch, but Denise, the young woman who's been painting with the group, mentioned that Greta Bailey has been very jealous of Letty's success. Apparently Letty's career was really taking off, leaving Greta, who had high hopes for her own budding career, in the dust. Denise also shed a little light on the relationship between Darren and Letty. Mind you, Denise is a loquacious, somewhat gossipy woman, so I can't vouch for anything she said, but according to her, Darren and Letty had an on-again, off-again relationship. This is also according to Denise," I prequalified the information. "Apparently, Darren took the art class just to be closer to Letty. And this all brings me to a slight confession."

Briggs looked up from his notes.

"I sort of, kind of, might have let it slip that Letty was murdered. Like Roger, most of the people who watched from across the street had concluded that Letty slipped on those treacherous rocks."

His lopsided grin appeared as he returned to his notepad. "What was that again? Sort of, kind of, might have? And can I quote you on that?"

"Funny man. I guess hunger makes you ornery."

He closed the notebook. "Yes, and I'm late. Hilda is going to give me an earful. Thanks for all your help today, Miss Pinkerton."

"You're very welcome, Detective Briggs."

CHAPTER 19

*I*t was an extraordinary spring day, and I had every intention of riding my bike to the shop until a text came through from Briggs.

"Morning, Miss Pinkerton, is there any chance you could stop by the station before you open up the shop? I need you to look at something."

"Absolutely."

Naturally, I was thrilled to help out on the case, thrilled enough that I rolled my bicycle back into the garage and pulled my car keys out of my backpack. I shaded my eyes and searched the trees for Kingston. He had flown off when he saw me push the bicycle out of the garage. The bird always danced and chattered happily when he saw that I was riding my bike to work. It meant he could take a leisurely flight around town, staying somewhat parallel with me while I rode down to Harbor Lane. I hoped he wouldn't be too confused when he didn't see me on my bicycle.

I climbed into the car and kept a watchful eye out for my crow as I drove to town. When a group of sparrows twittered up from a tree like kernels of popcorn in hot oil, I knew where my bird had landed.

I reached the police station and climbed out of the car. Briggs was just crossing back from the town square with the puppy. The dog rolled into a lope when he saw me waiting at the station. Briggs' shoes smacked the sidewalk as he took long, fast steps to keep his shoulder from being yanked from the socket.

I rubbed the dog's head between my hands. "Hey, good boy, I see you're taking the nice detective for a walk."

"Isn't that the truth." Briggs muttered as he opened the door for me. "I need wheels on my shoes."

Hilda peered up over the counter. She had made her usual sweet but sad attempt at adding a bit of color to the drab police station by taping a paper garland of tulips along the top edge of the counter. Several of the flowers had been ripped and repaired. Something told me the puppy might have been the culprit. The dog hopped up on his back legs and slapped the counter with his meaty front paws.

"Oh," Hilda squeaked, "I see my big friend is back."

"Yes, sorry, Hilda," Briggs apologized. "I don't think I can trust him alone at home. Any calls on the flyer?"

Hilda grinned. "Yes, one woman called." Her enthusiasm faded. "But she said she couldn't take him if he was going to be bigger than a beagle. That's what she has now, and she said she didn't want to give the beagle an inferiority complex. Anyhow, that puppy passed beagle size a few inches ago, and it seems he has many inches to go, so that was the end of that."

I followed Briggs and the dog through the counter gate. The puppy walked over and curled up on a nice, plush dog pillow in the corner behind Hilda's desk.

"Wow, someone has a nice bed." I looked at Briggs, who was trying to avoid direct eye contact.

"It was on sale at the store," he said rapidly.

"I see. So, what was it you wanted me to look at?"

"Follow me into the evidence room." We walked down the hallway to the back rooms. "I actually need your nose." He unlocked the door, and we entered the cold, stark evidence room.

"Maybe Hilda should put up a few paper tulips in this room," I said. "It's so uninviting in here, it sends a chill down my spine."

"Well, it isn't really meant to be a room for a tea party or Sunday brunch." He walked to the shelf and pulled down a box. "As I was packing the evidence bags away yesterday afternoon, I noticed that the bag holding the knife had gotten greasy with some sort of substance. If the rain washed away the blood, then it stands to reason that the substance left on the knife and in turn on the bag was a waterproof substance."

"Like a hand lotion or something?"

"That would be my guess." He placed the bag on the table. The plastic was smeared with a thin film of grease. "The lab will come by to swab the substance, but I thought I could get a quicker analysis from Samantha." He came close to tapping my nose with his finger, but stopped short of touching it. Oddly enough, I was disappointed.

I pulled on the latex gloves needed to examine evidence. "I don't think I'll need to take the knife out. I can just open the bag and take a whiff." I put the bag over my face to block out any other smells and took several deep breaths. There was more than enough residue for me to detect the fragrance of the greasy substance.

I pulled the bag away from my face. "Definitely a cosmetic preparation of some sort. Lotions usually contain glycerin that acts as a humectant. That helps keep moisture in as well as out. That's why the grease was still on the handle after the rain. Glycerin in itself doesn't have an odor, but we can see it on the bag. I'm sure the lab will confirm it. But to be more effective and, frankly, more pleasant, hand lotions generally contain an emollient, a fat or lipid of some kind and preferably one with a nice fragrance. According to my nose, the killer used a moisturizer with coconut oil. It's a popular scent for lotions and creams, not too sweet and very subtle."

"Do you know which brands contain coconut oil?"

"Not off hand but I think I'd be able to recognize this one if I smelled it somewhere other than the evidence bag."

"That's good to know." Briggs zipped the bag up.

"I'd say people who have their hands in paints and the solvents needed to thin them would need to constantly slather their hands in lotion to keep them from cracking. Just like florists." I showed him my own red knuckles. "Even then, it doesn't always do the trick."

"What hand lotion do you use?"

"I prefer one that is odor free. Otherwise, all I can smell when I'm eating is the lotion."

"Yes, that makes perfect sense." He carried the bag back to the shelf. "I'm going to be heading out to Jodie Dean's house this morning. If there's any way you can get away for an hour or two, it'd be nice to have you along. You know, just to sniff around."

"Your teacher? Is she a suspect?" I hadn't even considered the art teacher.

"No, not at all, but I need to interview each of the last people to see Letty. And Ms. Dean is on that list. I have to find out where each person went after the diner and gather alibis. I haven't taken any of the art class attendees off the list yet. And, as you said, artists would most likely be frequent users of hand lotion."

"So you want me to come as a partner in your investigation?"

Briggs smile was faint. We'd had more than one debate about whether or not I was his actual partner. As far as I was concerned, I was, even if it was mostly my nose that was involved in the investigation.

"I suppose if it makes you happy to think you're my partner, then I can consider you that."

I cupped my ear with my hand. "I'm sorry. I didn't quite hear that. You can consider me what?"

He tilted his head. Annoyance looked remarkably attractive on him. "Partner. Miss Pinkerton, would you like to come along as my temporary partner on this investigation?"

I pulled off my glove and stuck out my hand. "Not crazy about the 'temporary' adjective, but I'll take it."

Briggs hesitated before taking hold of my hand, and I realized it had nothing to do with the discussion. He stared at my hand for a second and then reached forward and wrapped his fingers around mine. His grasp was firm and confident, just like I expected. What I hadn't expected was a certain exchange of warmth from his palm and fingers to mine. As reluctantly as he took hold of my hand, he released it. A few seconds of awkward silence followed. which I quickly obliterated with a period of quick, successive claps.

"Yay, I'm an investigative partner. I've got to open the shop. What time do you need me back and reporting for duty?"

He led me out of the room and locked the door behind us. "I'll text you after the lab tech has come by to collect samples. Probably around ten."

"Perfect. See you then, partner." I turned around and saluted him.

"Guess I've really done it now."

CHAPTER 20

*R*yder shook his head with a quiet laugh as he lifted the bag of potting soil onto the work station.

"What's so amusing?" I asked, putting my attention back on the dull task of paperwork.

"Nothing much, except you've been gazing dreamy eyed out the windows all morning."

"Have I? I was just watching out for Kingston. He doesn't usually stay in the trees for so long."

"Well, he had a long weekend inside the house," Ryder reminded me. "And I don't think those starry eyed looks have anything to do with your crow."

I straightened and stacked the papers in front of me with more vigor than necessary. "Don't know what you're getting at. I'm just trying to puzzle out the murder mystery."

"Yes, the murder mystery you're solving with a certain detective."

I spun around to face him. "Did Lola put you up to this?"

"Lola? No, why did she say something about me?" he asked anxiously.

Now it was my turn to laugh and pat myself on the back for turning the conversation away from my starry eyed daydreams out the window. "No, it's just she's constantly needling me about Detective Briggs." I looked at my phone for the hundredth time to see if he'd texted yet. No word. Maybe he'd decided not to take me along on his interview after all. That notion sank my shoulders. But I straightened instantly when his text buzzed through.

"Will you still be able to go with me to Jodie Dean's house?"

"Yes," I texted back quickly.

"I'll swing by and pick you up."

"You don't even have to tell me." Ryder put up a soil covered hand. "I can tell by your expression. I'll hold down the fort while you're gone. Don't forget that Elsie needs my help after lunch with a delivery of ingredients."

"That's right. I'll make sure to be back by then." Detective Briggs pulled up in front of the shop. I grabbed my sweater and reached under the counter for my purse. Then I tried unsuccessfully to push a few errant curls from my forehead and hurried to the door.

"Remember," Ryder said, stopping my progress. "Try not to look too excited. Play it cool."

"Oh shush, you ornery shop assistant and finish planting that basil." I rushed out the door but then heeded Ryder's advice. I was acting like a teenage girl waiting for her first mad crush to pick her up for ice cream. I was merely assisting Detective Briggs on a murder inquiry. There was no mad crush or future prospect of ice cream. (Well, maybe a mild crush.)

Detective Briggs, always the gentleman, stepped out to open the passenger door. "Good morning, partner," I semi-sang as I slid into the seat.

"Good morning, Miss Pinkerton." He shut the door and walked around to the driver's side.

"Where are we going first?" I opened my purse and pulled out the notebook and pen Briggs had given me on Valentine's Day. Most women would have grimaced at the lack of romance in a notebook and pen, but I secretly loved the gift. It was just like his, and as far as I was concerned, it was his subtle way of telling me he enjoyed my company on his investigations. Even more importantly, it meant he considered me to be a serious detective, like himself. Even if I wasn't wearing a badge.

Briggs took a sideways glance at the notebook and tamped down a smile. "I see you came prepared."

I patted the notebook on my lap. "Yep. These pages have been far too blank. They were in need of a good murder." I pulled my mouth down at the sides. "Oops, that sounded terrible. Obviously there is no such thing as a *good* murder."

"That's all right. I understood the context. And to answer your first question, we are heading to Jodie Dean's house in Mayfield. I'm hoping she can give me some insight into the various interrelationships of the art group. I thought she might know some of Letty's outside friends and acquaintances, as well."

"So she's not a person of interest? I thought she was with Letty the night she disappeared."

"Well, yes, of course. I need to find out what she did after dinner with Letty. But I hadn't thought much about her as a person of interest."

"Oh? Why is that? Is it because she was your teacher, and she helped save your diploma?"

His chin shifted back and forth as he adjusted the rearview mirror. "Hmm, I guess that's a good question. Maybe I subconsciously took her off the list because of that. Still, she seems like an unlikely suspect. By the way, the lab technician came by and collected a swab from the inside the evidence bag. He said they have a database to match chemical compounds to a specific cosmetic brand. He also said the tests could take up to three days. I thought maybe you could get us closer to the specific brand and the user of that brand and in less time."

"I'll do my sneaky, sniffy best," I said confidently.

CHAPTER 21

*J*odie Dean graciously invited us into her home, a midcentury ranch house on a quiet street. Exactly the house you would expect a teacher to live in. She was wearing a painter's smock and had short curls clipped up off her face and neck. There were two paintbrushes in her hand, both coated with yellow paint.

"If you don't mind, I'm just cleaning up." We followed her through the front room into the kitchen. She stepped out onto a service porch to clean the brushes. "If I don't rinse them now, they'll be ruined. And they don't look like much, but they cost a pretty penny." She spoke loudly over the sound of water rushing into the utility sink.

Briggs and I stood in the kitchen while she finished cleaning the brushes. A coffee pot beeped four times, letting us know the brewing session was done.

"Would you like some coffee?" Jodie called from the service porch.

"No, thank you," Briggs answered.

A round table was situated in the corner of the kitchen, beneath a window and in front of a tall cabinet filled with tea pots and porcelain trinkets. Mail was spread out on one side of the table. I couldn't help but notice that there was more than one piece of mail with the dreaded pink insert, a business or utilities' way of letting you know your payment was overdue. Pink was usually the final color before the creditors knocked on your door. It seemed that Jodie Dean was having some financial difficulties. I waved my hand in the direction of the mail. Briggs nodded that he'd seen the overdue notices too.

"Is she married?" I whispered.

He shook his head. "I think they divorced when I was still in high school," he said quietly and finished just as the sink turned off.

Jodie came around the corner wiping her hands on a towel. They were, not surprisingly, red and chapped. "You'd think I had to wash up for surgery everyday with the way these hands look. Which reminds me—"

Briggs and I exchanged questioning looks as she disappeared down the hallway. She returned a few seconds later, rubbing white lotion between her hands. "I finally got a prescription lotion from the doctor. I think the over-the-counter stuff was making my hands worse." She showed off her red knuckles and cracked fingertips. "This stuff already feels much better, like my skin is drinking it in."

Jodie let out a sad breath, and her shoulders lifted and fell. Her demeanor changed dramatically. "I can't tell you how distraught I am over the news. Letty was a good person with a promising career ahead of her. That's why I was painting this morning. It always takes my mind off things." As she spoke, her eyes flitted to the table. Apparently she realized that she'd left her late notice bills out for us to see. She walked over and swept everything into a pile and pushed it into a drawer in the trinket cabinet. "Now what can I help you with, James? Excuse me, Detective Briggs. I just can't get used to that. It seems so formal." She was a pleasant enough person, and it seemed she still felt some nostalgic connection to her past students. Jodie favored me with a polite smile.

"Yes, Ms. Dean, I believe you've met my friend Lacey Pinkerton. Miss Pinkerton has a specialized skill that lends itself occasionally to an investigation."

Her lips pursed together. "Is that right? I can hardly imagine what skill that might be." She was fishing for information, but Briggs made it clear that he'd said all he planned to say on the matter.

Briggs pulled out his notebook. "As I mentioned on the phone, I was hoping to get a little more insight into the relationships Letty Clark had with the other artists. And while we're at it, I need to write down your account of the evening. When you last saw Letty and where you went afterward."

Jodie's lips pursed again. "I don't see how that will help but that's fine. Are you sure neither of you wants coffee?" She pulled a cup down from the cupboard.

"No, thank you," I said. "I've already had several cups this morning. In fact, if you don't mind, could I use your bathroom? I hate to be a bother but—"

"Of course, dear. Then James and I can have our little chat. First door on the right."

I headed down the short hallway to the first door. Since she had just used it, Jodie's hand lotion was on the counter. It had a pharmacy label taped to it with instructions to rub liberally on hands three to four times a day or after washing. I lifted the bottle. There was still a globule left on the tip. I took a deep whiff and was not surprised to find it odorless. A prescription strength hand cream wouldn't have any of the same frilly, fragrant additives as the over-the-counter product. This lotion was the real thing. It was meant to heal chapped hands. I placed the bottle back on the same spot and made a point of flushing and washing my hands.

Jodie seemed to prefer a private talk with Briggs, so I lingered in the bathroom, not wanting to interrupt whatever it was she had to tell him. I quietly smelled a few of the other cosmetics sitting on the counter. There was a face powder and some lipstick, but nothing had a coconut oil scent. I finished up my pretend restroom stop and made sure to walk loudly along the hallway, letting them know I was on my way back to the kitchen.

Briggs was writing something down in his notebook. My return had taken Jodie's attention off the discussion. She smiled and hopped up from the table. "I nearly forgot, my friend sent me some delicious Italian cookies." She walked to a bright blue and white cookie jar and pulled it out from beneath the cabinet. "They are so delicious with a touch of anise. I can't stop eating them."

"I'm fine," Briggs said as he pushed up from the chair and put his notebook away.

"No, thank you," I said. "And thank you for letting me use your restroom."

Jodie's rounded gaze shot to Briggs. "Is that it then? Well, that didn't take too long. I'll be able to get back to my work."

"Yes, thank you," Briggs said. "And I apologize for taking up your time this morning."

Jodie led us to the front door. "I do hope you get to the bottom of this tragedy soon. At least so her parents can have closure. And her friends, of course," she added rather awkwardly at the end.

Briggs and I headed out to the car and climbed inside. We both looked at each other, hoping there was news to share.

I shook my head. "No match on the hand lotion. Although, I'm sure you knew that your favorite teacher would not be involved."

"A comedian with a cute and helpful nose."

"I will take that list as a compliment. What did you find out or did you spend the time reminiscing about your high school glory days?"

"Trust me, they weren't all that glorious." He started the car and pulled out onto the road. "Jodie Dean gave me a few of the same details you learned from Denise. Letty and Darren had a somewhat tumultuous relationship that she seemed to think leaned more toward Darren wanting to keep it going and Letty wanting it over for good."

"Did it seem as if Ms. Dean suspected that Darren might have had something to do with her death?"

"I did get that sense. But she also brought up how angry Greta Bailey has been about Letty's sudden success. Greta has been trying for some time to get noticed by collectors, and Letty sort of flew right past her."

"That confirms everything Denise told me. Sounds like you have some motives, anyhow."

"Yes, it's a start. Thank you for taking time away from the shop to help me with this. I'm going to head back to the station. While we were in the house, I got a text from the coroner's office. He said the initial analysis was in."

"And I need to cover the store while Ryder helps Elsie with a delivery."

"Is the bakery up and running again?"

"Sort of. I don't think Elsie had too many goodies to offer today, but she said she felt much better. She'll be back at a hundred percent soon enough. Otherwise, I'm afraid Port Danby will suffer from baked good withdrawals."

CHAPTER 22

*R*yder brought back a plate of chocolate chip scones. "From Elsie. One for me for helping and one for you for letting me help."

"I thought she was going to take it easy on baking today," I noted but didn't let my worry for Elsie's health stop me from taking a bite of the flaky scone. Elsie had put a dollop of whipped butter on each scone and it dripped down the sides like butter on a stack of hotcakes. Only the scone was far better than pancakes.

I dabbed at my lip to keep the melted butter from running down my chin. "Hmm, so good. And just in time. My stomach was growling, and I'm almost sure I heard it roar the words chocolate chip scone during its hunger tantrum." Kingston clattered his claws along his perch, letting me know he needed some kind of treat as well. I pulled out the can of dog treats, his new favorite, and walked over to give him a few.

Ryder stretched his arms back. "Those bags of flour are heavy. Like bags of flour," he laughed. "As much as I love the scones, I'm in need of something a little meatier. I was going to go buy a burger and take a break."

"Absolutely. You earned it."

Ryder grabbed his beanie from the hook and pushed it down over his head, causing his long bangs to nearly cover his eyes. "Do you want anything?"

"Nope, I'm good with the scone. Have a good lunch." Kingston quickly finished the treats. As I handed him a third one, Detective Briggs walked inside with the puppy.

"I could swear he's grown since I saw him. When was that, this morning?" I tossed the dog a treat.

"Sometimes I think he's growing right before my eyes. Hilda needed a break, so I decided to take him for a walk to see if I could take out some of that nonstop energy."

"To do that, I think you'll need to run at full speed up to the Hawksworth Manor and back. Twice." I gave both the dog and the bird one more treat and walked back to the work island to hide the can from my very clever crow. "What did the coroner have to say?"

"The knife wound hit a major artery. Mercifully, it seemed she was dead before the killer shoved her body into the storm surge. He thinks she died pretty close to midnight."

"Which means that it happened soon after they left the diner."

Briggs pulled out his notepad. A receipt fell out of it. "It's the bill from their late night dinner. Franki made a copy and let me have the original. The receipt says 11:40. The server was Franki's son, Tyler. He remembered serving the group. He said they left about ten minutes after he handed them the bill."

"And what about Letty's phone. Was it ruined by the rain?"

"I've got some tech experts working on it. They are trying to bring it back from death by drowning." He pushed the receipt back into his notepad. "Greta Bailey works at a bank in Chesterton. She's off at four. I told her I needed to ask her a few questions about that night. I'm meeting her at her house at five. I'm hoping she can tell us about her knife purchase too."

He walked over to say hello to Kingston but got too close with the dog and caused a storm of black feathers. The flapping of wings caused the dog to bolt backwards. Briggs had a good laugh. "He's entertaining, that's for sure."

"I think you'll miss him when he's gone."

"No. I'll notice him missing, but I won't miss him," he stated emphatically, but I wasn't convinced. "I better take him for one more loop around the town. I did want to ask though . . ."

"Yes, I would like to go along when you interview Greta Bailey."

"All right then. I'll pick you up on my way to Chesterton. And thanks for the dog treats." He stopped at the door. "Sure you don't want a dog? I hear they go great with crows."

"Oh, is that what you hear? What about imperialistic cats?"

"Sure. I think Nevermore would welcome him with open paws."

"See you later, Detective Briggs."

"Good bye, Miss Pinkerton."

CHAPTER 23

I pulled my notebook and pen out of my purse. "Ready when you are, sir," I said with my deepest, most serious tone.

"We don't want to scare the woman off with a notebook assault. Maybe you should leave yours in the car and just figure out how to take a sniff of her hand lotion, like you so cleverly did at Ms. Dean's house."

"I think you might be overstating the cleverness of that scheme. Needing to use a bathroom is fairly standard practice for women. I didn't need to dig too deeply into my box of creative ideas to come up with it. Might even try it again in Greta's house."

We stepped out of the car in front of the pale blue house with contrasting black shutters. A charming brick path led up to a porch that had been transformed into a jungle by a plethora of ferns, palms and potted rubber plants.

My eyes swept around the lush yard. "Looks like Greta has a green thumb along with her artist's eye."

"I think this is the owner's house. Greta rents the back house."

I followed Briggs to a back gate. He reached over and unlocked it. The lush, dense landscaping ended halfway across the yard and faded into pockmarked cement and a much less charming brick pathway. Around every fourth brick was missing, leaving the pathway a maze of ankle twisting opportunities.

The back house looked like the sad, lonely stepsister of the front house with faded gray shutters that hung crooked on a pale blue facade.

"Apparently pride of ownership stopped right there in the middle of the yard," I muttered as I carefully navigated the treacherous brick pathway.

Greta was anticipating Detective Briggs' visit. She opened the front door before we reached the stoop. The scent of grilled onions wafted out, reminding me that I'd only had a chocolate scone for the entire day. The aroma was quickly followed by the distinct, less pleasant smell of cat litter.

"You'll have to excuse the mess," Greta said before we stepped inside. "After the terrible events of the weekend and then having to drag myself to work today, I just didn't have the energy or will to pick up the house."

I noticed immediately that Greta's face was much more pale and drawn than Jodie's. She looked like a woman who had just lost an acquaintance to a horrible murder. Whereas, Jodie seemed much more together and rested. Of course, that meant nothing, but I was planning to write about the observation in my notebook once I got back to the car.

"Ms. Bailey, I think you've met Miss Pinkerton. She is my assistant on this case."

I preferred partner but assistant wasn't too shabby either.

"Yes, we've met before. Good to see you again." I lifted my hand forward, hoping for a handshake. She hesitated, then awkwardly took my hand for a half-hearted shake. Her palm and fingers were dry and chapped. I didn't sense any lotion.

As Greta turned to lead us into the gloomy front room, I pressed my fingers to my nose and breathed deeply. I pulled them away quickly. Fresh cut onions. I blinked to keep my eyes from watering.

"I was just making myself some dinner. Can I offer you a beverage?" Greta asked.

"A glass of water, if you don't mind," Briggs said. I knew he was less interested in quenching his thirst and more interested in getting a view of the kitchen where sets of knives would be kept. As we stepped into the kitchen, two cats shot past us leaving behind their food dishes.

I glanced back as their long tails disappeared around the corner of the hallway. "I think we disturbed their dinner."

"They'll be back," Greta said. "Probably before we walk out of here. Not much stands between Tommy and Pete and their cat chow."

I laughed. "I think I have their long lost brother at home."

Greta seemed to warm up to me faster than Jodie had but then cat owners always had a connection. While we were caught up in a quick exchange of cat stories, Briggs took a short stroll around the kitchen. From the corner of my eye, I could see him looking at the knife set. It was the set with the mother-of pearl inlay on the handles. Three slots were empty. A knife was sitting on the cutting board next to some cut broccoli.

"Ms. Bailey," Briggs said, cutting short our cat stories. "Did you buy this knife set at the flea market? I thought I saw one just like it when I strolled through the tables."

Greta looked a little perplexed by the question. "Why yes, I did. Aren't they beautiful? Unfortunately, one of the knives was missing, so the man, a retired chef, Roger, I think, sold it to me for half price. He was thoroughly disappointed to let it go for such a low price. He said the set was complete when he brought it to the flea market."

Briggs looked at the knife on the cutting board. "I see you're missing more than one. This big slot is usually for the bread cutting knife."

"Yes," she said sounding more agitated than she had a few minutes earlier. "I—I used it earlier." She walked over to the sink and picked up an extra long, serrated knife. "I was just about to wash it."

"Excuse me," I interrupted, "could I use your restroom. I had an extra large soda at lunch." I wasn't sure why I needed to add the detail of my liquid intake to give weight to my bathroom use, especially after what I'd told Briggs in the car.

"Yes, it's right around the corner." I left the discussion and made my way to the bathroom to do my nosing around in Greta's cosmetics for hand lotion. I discovered long before I reached the door, that the bathroom was where she kept her cat litter box and it needed cleaning. Growing up, I'd learned to block or tone down strong smells so that I could eat foods without smelling everything around me. I had to really work to employ those skills as I stood in her bathroom trying not to succumb to the overwhelming odor of the cat box. Nevermore didn't know how lucky he was having an owner with an extra sensitive nose. His litter box was always pristine.

I quickly searched through the few cosmetic items on the counter and in drawers, trying not to disturb anything. If Greta did use hand lotion, she didn't keep it in the bathroom. It could be a number of places like her car or bedroom or with her art supplies. Or it was possible she didn't use any at all. Some people didn't care for the greasy feel of moisturizer on their skin. Whatever the reason, it seemed I was not going to be much help to Detective Briggs this round.

I headed out just as Briggs was finishing up.

Greta seemed agitated with the line of questioning. She was wearing a stony mask as she spoke. "I don't understand, why would

I need someone to witness that I came straight home after dinner? Am I under suspicion? Why don't you find out where Darren Morgan went afterward? He's the one you need to be badgering with these questions."

One thing I'd learned about Detective Briggs was that he rarely, if ever, lost his cool, and he was exceptionally good at placating witnesses who felt instantly scrutinized by his interview.

"You're not under suspicion, Ms. Bailey," he assured her in his deep, smooth voice. "I'm conducting a murder investigation, and the first stage of that is to talk to the last people to see the victim. I'm just trying to ascertain where people were at the time of the murder. I assure you, everyone else in the dinner party, including Mr. Morgan, will be receiving the same string of questions."

Greta shuffled her feet some and physically shook off some of the ire. "I suppose that makes sense. Well, I came straight home to an empty house, with only my cats as witnesses." A nervous laugh followed.

"What about the people in the front house?" Briggs asked. "Would they have seen or heard you come in?"

A dry laugh shot from her mouth. "They are in their late eighties. They wouldn't hear me unless I was standing right in front of them waving my arms and yelling 'I'm home'. Besides, they are generally in bed before nine."

Briggs folded up his notebook. "Thank you for your cooperation, Ms. Bailey."

"How did she die? Is it certain that she was murdered?" Greta asked as she walked us to the door.

Briggs cleared his throat, his go-to stalling tactic when he was deciding how much to say. "We know she was murdered. Don't worry. We will find her killer soon. Good evening, Ms. Bailey."

We climbed into the car.

"Any luck on the hand lotion?" Briggs asked as he turned the ignition.

"No, unfortunately and the handshake was a bust too, especially after she'd been chopping onions." I turned slightly sideways in my seat to look at him. "I know I'm pretty new at this detective stuff, but did you think she acted sort of strange when you asked her about the knives?"

"Guilty of something, you mean?" Briggs asked.

"I noticed the hesitation and tripping over words." He flashed me a look that I could only describe as proud.

"You're a quick learner."

"Thanks. Another thing I noticed was her irate reaction to your questions about her whereabouts after the dinner."

"That reaction is more common than you might imagine. People immediately think they are being accused. It's a natural defense, and almost more so with people who had nothing at all to do with the murder and didn't even consider the question might be asked. It catches them off guard because they know they did nothing wrong. But guilty people react that way too. Her reaction was a wash, typical for guilty or innocent."

I pulled out my notebook. "I'm going to write those pearls of wisdom down if you don't mind. I'm a fast learner, but I also have a good teacher." As I fished around in my purse for a pen, my fingers grazed a small sample of hand lotion I'd picked up at the store. It had a wonderful lavender scent, but I'd found it too greasy to use anywhere except just before bed. The hand cream pushed another thought into my mind.

"Detective Briggs, is it possible that the cream on the knife handle came from Letty? What if she struggled with her assailant and even managed, at some point, to get her hand around the knife handle? Then we're spending a lot of time looking for evidence that won't do us any good, even when we find it. I took a brief smell inventory of Letty's cosmetics when we thought we were looking for a missing person. Aside from a perfume that I recognized mostly as bergamot, the rest of the scents are sort of jumbled in my head. I didn't realize they'd come into play again."

Briggs looked over at me. "Well done," he said before turning his eyes back to the road. "I've instructed the coroner to check for traces of hand lotion on the victim's hands so we can see if it matches the substance found on the knife. In the meantime, I thought we'd swing by Letty's house once more and have another look around. Then you can get that stellar nose of yours on the job and beat the coroner and the lab techs to the conclusion."

"Perfect." I sat back with satisfaction. "Guess I'm really thinking like a detective now."

"I guess so."

CHAPTER 24

The last time Briggs and I had visited Letty Clark's house, she was only a missing person and we were looking for clues that would help us locate her. Now we were hoping to find something that would lead us to her killer. Nothing much had changed at the house. Weeds still cluttered the front yard and paint was still peeling off the facade. But knowing that the house was empty because the person living there had been killed, made the whole place look especially lonely.

"I guess I'd better take the spare key to the station this time," Briggs said as he lifted the front edge of the pot. He reached under for the key but couldn't find it right away. He leaned the pot over farther, nearly spilling the dry soil over the lip as he felt around for the key. "Got it." He held it up triumphantly and lowered the pot.

I stared down at the frazzled, dead remnants of the plant. "Has someone come to inspect the house since we were here?"

Briggs wasn't sure what I was getting at but instead of questioning me, he pulled out his notebook to give me a verified answer. He flipped through a few pages. "Just making sure. No, I haven't sent anyone to the house since then. We were focused on the murder location at Pickford Beach. Why do you ask?"

"Because I'm the one who placed the key back under the pot. I remember thinking if Letty had abandoned her car, then it was probable that she had misplaced her keys. And if she got back home, I wanted to make sure she had a key to get inside. When I put the key back, I barely tipped the pot and set the key right under the front edge."

The questioning lines smoothed from his brow. "I had to tip the pot all the way back to get to the key, which means someone else used it since our last visit."

"Seems like the only explanation. Maybe her parents came by."

"No, they were delayed in London. Bad weather cancelled their flight to New York. They're expected back tomorrow. It's possible a friend came by."

Briggs pushed the key in the door and we stepped inside. The chemical fumes had dissipated since our last visit. It took me only a few seconds to shake off the effects.

"I'm going straight in to smell her hand lotion. The last time we were here I was concentrating on her perfume, a scent that I assumed would be on her clothes. But I took only a cursory sniff of the hand lotion." I headed through to the postage stamp sized bathroom. There were actually two types of skin cream, one that could be applied after a shower and one for chapped, dry skin. One had the faint nutty smell of shea butter and the other was packed with citric acid, oatmeal, lavender oils and every fragrance that could be squeezed into a bottle of lotion. The one fragrance that was missing was coconut.

"Miss Pinkerton, come see this," Briggs called from another room.

I hurried through the house and found him standing in the back room Letty had been using as an art studio.

"Oh wow," I said on a gasp as my gaze circled the room. Every one of Letty's paintings, including the unfinished jacarandas on the easel, had been slashed. The artwork had been damaged beyond repair. A large deep slice had split Darren Morgan's face in two." I walked up to it. "Why on earth would someone destroy this art? How horribly cruel for someone to take a life and then erase the legacy of that life along with it." I glanced back at Briggs. He was examining the back side of some of the paintings leaning haphazardly against the walls in the room.

"Was it a knife?" I asked.

"I'd say a good sharp one at that."

"Like one that could cut through a crusty loaf of bread?"

He knew exactly what I was getting at. "Could be. But we can't automatically connect the destruction of artwork to Letty's murder."

"Obviously. But we know that Greta Bailey was jealous of Letty's quick rise to stardom in the art world."

"Yes but if Letty is dead, the competition is too. Why would Greta need to destroy the work?"

"Ah ha, I know the answer to that. Because after an artist dies, their—"

"Their artwork becomes even more sought after," Briggs finished enthusiastically for me.

I blew out a deflated sigh. "You just took the wind out of my ah-ha moment."

"Sorry. But you are right." He winked. "As usual."

"That flattery won't get you anywhere after stealing my moment. Although, I guess it helps a little."

"Let's take a look through the rest of the rooms to see if anything else was vandalized."

I followed close at his heels, suddenly feeling a little uneasy in the house knowing that someone had been inside with a knife doing damage.

The house was quite small. It was easy to see that most everything was untouched since our last inspection. We headed past the bathroom to the bedroom.

"Oh, that's right. We got sidetracked by the slashed paintings. No luck on the hand lotion. The fragrances don't match the substance on the knife handle."

"Good to know." He pushed open the bedroom door.

I noticed instantly that something was different. I walked to the dresser. The porcelain face of the doll was in the awkward tilt I'd left it in after it had popped off in my hand. But the painting that Letty had purchased from Fiona Diggle was gone.

"The flea market painting with the mountain lupines was sitting right here." I tapped the dresser.

"Yes, I remember." He walked forward and stooped to pick up the business card from the auction house. "It seems the thief brushed this off the dresser in their hurry to run off with the painting." He read the card. "Joseph Morgan, auctioneer," Briggs read. "I wonder if he's related to Darren Morgan." He pulled out his notebook and pushed the card inside. "Didn't you say that Jodie Dean was interested in that painting?"

"Yes, Letty thought it might be worth something, but Jodie dismissed the idea. Later that day, Jodie came back looking for it, but Letty had already bought it."

"Interesting." He looked around. "Well, I think we're done here. I'll file a report on the vandalism in the house. I'll keep the spare key at the station. If someone needs to get into the house, they'll have to come to me first."

We walked out the front door.

"All in all, a successful afternoon, eh, partner?" I asked.

"Not bad. But it'll be more successful when we find the killer."

CHAPTER 25

The morning and early afternoon had come and gone quickly. Ryder had taken the morning off for his mom's birthday. He had treated her to breakfast and shopping. In the meantime, every person within a fifty mile radius had decided it was a great day to order or buy flowers. The final flurry of customers had slowed an hour before Ryder arrived.

"Busy day, boss?" he asked.

I showcased the extreme clutter and mess on the island with a wave of my arm. "Either that, or a hurricane moved through this morning, leaving this disaster behind." I patted a stack of new orders. "Boss lady did good today. And I already ordered the extra blooms we need to fill the new orders. I'm not sure what happened, but apparently everyone within driving distance of Port Danby woke up deciding they needed flowers. Not that I'm complaining. How was your mom's special day? I wish you would have just taken the entire day, then you wouldn't have had to rush back."

"That's all right. I need the hours anyhow. I let my mom pick her gift." He moved his head side to side. "Let's just say a lot of my past birthday gifts never left the hanger or box. Some even mysteriously found their way back to the store. So I told her I'd take her out to pick her own gift. I had no idea purses were so expensive."

"They are kind of ridiculous."

"Ridiculous? I swear one shop offered low interest financing for their designer handbags. Women take out loans to buy something that is meant to hold their money. I'd say that's a hair past ridiculous. But she was happy, and she's worth it."

"That's sweet, Ryder. And I know about the gift conundrum. Can't tell you how many times I excitedly handed my mom a beautifully wrapped gift, sure she would be over the moon about it, only to have her force a quick smile and say, 'well, isn't that lovely'."

Kingston, who had been glued to his perch during the mad rush of customers, swept through the air and landed on the island. He scooted close enough to Ryder for a head scratch.

"Anyhow, I'm here now, if you want to take a lunch break."

I grabbed my sweater off the hook. "I ate a yogurt and banana in between customers, but I need to drive into Mayfield. The craft store got in more of those glass beads we need for the party bouquets. I should be back in an hour."

"All right. And don't forget to pick up some more pastel ribbon for the tulips. We're running low on yellow and pink."

"Right. Ribbon." I headed out the door.

I hadn't seen or heard from Briggs since he dropped me off at my car the night before. I was sure he was busy with the case. I tried not to feel insulted that he hadn't filled me in on any new developments. I decided a quick text to see if there were any updates wouldn't hurt. I was, after all, his ad hoc partner on this investigation.

"Anything new on the case?" I typed and then quickly replaced *the* with *our* for no other reason except it was fun to tease him.

I'd climbed into my car and put on my seatbelt before his text came back. "I'm at the Mayfield court house waiting to testify. Previous case. Going back into the courtroom now."

"Have fun." I texted back and put away the phone.

I drove east out of Port Danby toward Mayfield. Mayfield was bigger and more populated than Port Danby. It had a lot more specialty stores, like the craft shop where I occasionally shopped for ribbons, glass beads and decorative vases. I turned up Parson Drive, the street that cut through the commercial district. Millie's Crafts and Hobbies was at the end of the street. Parking spots were often hard to come by, especially in the middle of the day. It seemed today was no different.

I waited patiently for a woman to vacate a spot that was only a block away from the craft shop. She had several shopping bags, and she took her time making sure they were set just right in the trunk. She glanced back at me more than once, sort of teasing me with her slow movements, almost as if she knew she had something valuable and that she was not inclined to give it up too easily or quickly. I cast her one of my tight lipped smiles to let her know I would wait even if she decided to check air pressure and oil before backing out of the spot. I had pulled to the side enough to leave plenty of room for other drivers to go past, but many raced by with glowers, pretending I'd inconvenienced them when I knew darn well their rage came from not being first at the spot. I waved cheerily to all the scowling drivers.

As I waited, the door to Urban Antiques opened and a woman walked out carrying a painting. It was Jodie Dean. She carried the painting carelessly in her hand as if she was ready to heave it at the first person who looked at her wrong. I pushed up straighter in my seat to get a better look at the canvas as she strode past on the sidewalk. It was Fiona Diggle's mountain lupine painting.

I'd been concentrating on the art, but as I looked up, I met Jodie's agitated gaze. She looked quickly away.

I smacked the steering wheel. "That's where the painting went."

That sneaky, thoughtless woman must have decided that since Letty was dead, she wouldn't need her flea market purchase.

I adjusted my rearview mirror toward the parked cars. Jodie's car was several spaces back. Unlike my friend in the Cadillac, Jodie wasted no time. She unceremoniously threw the painting into the trunk and slammed it shut. Jodie was definitely angry about something.

The Cadillac driver had run out of stalling moves. She backed out and I pulled into the spot. I quickly pulled my phone from my purse. I'd heard of Urban Antiques, mostly because Lola mentioned that her parents were good friends with the owner, Rick Urban. I rang up Lola.

"Hey, Pink, just got in the coolest box of men's hats."

"I'm sure that made your day. I was calling to ask you a question. Are you free to talk a second?"

"Yep, the store is as quiet as a graveyard."

"I'm parked in front of Urban Antiques."

"Traitor."

"I'm not buying anything. In fact, I'm not even going inside the store."

A honk jarred me out of my thoughts. I looked through the back window. A grumpy man in a truck was motioning for me to pull out, apparently thinking I was leaving. I waved him past. "My gosh, the parking spots in Mayfield are like winning lotto tickets," I quipped. "Back to my question. You said you know the owner of Urban Antiques. By any far off chance, does he know something about art?"

"He sure does. Rick Urban used to work for some of the big museums in New York and France. He's an art expert."

"So if someone had a painting that they thought might have some value, he'd be a person to go to for an appraisal or to find out if it was authentic?"

"Absolutely. Twice, he had to deliver bad news to my mom

when she spent too much on art thinking it was the real deal only to find out it was fake. Now she knows to ask Rick first, buy second."

"Great. That tells me everything I need to know." I grabbed my purse.

"Why are you in Mayfield?"

"I need to get some things at the craft shop. If your business is slow, you should go across the street and visit Ryder."

"I should but I think I'll just stay here and try on dusty old man hats."

"All right then, have fun with that. And thanks for the info." I hung up and dropped my phone into my purse.

As I climbed out of the car, a lady yelled through her passenger window. "Are you leaving?"

I looked back at my car. "I was climbing out. Not in."

"Fine." She drove off, obviously very disgusted with my timing.

I headed down the block to the craft store. I had some interesting new tidbits to tell Detective Briggs. Jodie was in unexplained possession of Letty's painting. It seemed Ms. Dean had just helped herself to it. She might have been the one who moved the key. Did she slash the other paintings too? At some point in time, Jodie must have decided the artwork might be valuable. Only, from the way she carried it, like someone might carry a sack of potatoes, it seemed that her first inclination had been right. Her expression and mannerisms as she left the antique store indicated that she'd heard bad news from Rick Urban, the art expert. The real question was—how far had Jodie been willing to go to get her hands on that painting?

CHAPTER 26

The longer spring hours once again coaxed me out to the front yard for some gardening. Wanting to add some height and even more vivid color to the yard, I'd taken a cue from Marty Tate and picked up several pots of red and yellow snapdragons. My neighbor, Dash, had also taken advantage of the long daylight hours. He finished mowing the last stretch of his front lawn and shut down the motor.

"I guess the spring gardening bug has bitten my neighbor." He stepped over the small border shrub that separated our two yards. The smell of fresh cut grass brought up a sneeze. I put down the trowel and covered my face with my arm.

"Bless you. I think I caused that with my new aftershave scent, cut grass. Although, the yard is still more weeds than grass."

I stood up to get circulation moving in my legs again. "Marty Tate planted a bunch of snapdragons in front of the light keeper's cottage, so I decided they'd look good in front of my own cottage."

"Speaking of Marty and the lighthouse, I'm going to climb to the top tomorrow night. It's supposed to be an awesome full moon, and the forecast says clear skies. Are you up for a little adventure?"

"Hmm, sneaking into the lighthouse to watch the full moon sounds sort of teen-ish. Of course, I'm in. Anytime I can take myself back to the carefree, fun days of high school, I'm all for it. But one question. How are we going to get into the lighthouse?"

"Through the door," he said matter-of-factly.

"What about the lock?"

"Do you mean the lock that was broken by an adventurous youth long ago that Marty has never changed? To the uninformed eye, it looks locked. But one good yank and it pops open."

"I see. Boy, Marty might take good care of the lighthouse, but he's rather remiss on his lock system."

Dash clapped his hands together. "Perfect. So tomorrow night around ten. Or if that's too late—"

"Ten is fine. No self-respecting teen would sneak up there earlier than that. It would ruin the adventure. So, this adventurous youth, the lock breaker, would his initials happen to be D.V.?"

"Me?" He pretended to be insulted. "I would never do anything so wrong. It was some kid who graduated a good five years before I got to high school. His name was Garth and he was quite the legend for breaking into places. I think he's the one who made Hawksworth Manor the town's favorite teen hangout."

Just as he said it, a truck full of kids came down from Maple Hill.

"Until tomorrow night then." Dash headed back to his front yard. I waved to him as he pushed his lawn mower into the backyard.

I knelt down to my flowers. I had just enough light to finish the last two snapdragons. I was deep in thought about the day, the flurry of business and the many orders I had to fill in the coming week. Then there was the trip to Mayfield where I'd spotted Jodie with Letty's painting. I'd sent a quick text to Briggs to let him know that I had something interesting to tell him, but I hadn't heard back. He always had so much on his plate with the investigation and intermittent court appearances for past cases. He'd complained more than once that court days were his least favorite and the most grueling part of the job.

I drew the tip of my trowel along the root-bound base of the snapdragon plant and then slipped it into the soil. A noise that I was certain was human footsteps sounded from somewhere behind me.

"Did you change your mind about the moon?" I asked with a laugh as I spun around on my kneeling pad.

My front yard was empty. "Captain?" I called, but there was no sign of Dash's dog. I'd left Nevermore and Kingston inside so that I could finish the project before dark. I shrugged it off as either my imagination or a large squirrel wearing shoes.

Seconds later, I was rubbing a crawling sensation off the back of my neck. My yard was empty, but I couldn't help but feel that I was being watched. Deciding that low blood sugar was making me hear and feel things that weren't there, I hurried to finish the last plant. There was a leftover slice of pizza in my refrigerator just waiting to be melted back into stringy, gooey goodness in the microwave. I collected my things and went inside.

CHAPTER 27

*A*s I nibbled on the slice of pizza, I considered the possibility that I'd built up the tastiness of reheated mozzarella and pepperoni a bit too much in my mind. I dropped the rubbery crust into the trash. Headlights flashed along Maple Hill as a few more cars with loud music and laughter drove down from the manor. It seemed there had been quite a gathering up there this afternoon.

I'd been too busy to think about the Hawksworth murders and I'd had no time to visit the research room in the library. After Lola had shown me the secret key on the antique jewelry box, I wondered if the old chest in the gardener shed, the makeshift museum, had one of those secret keys. The items displayed for visitors interested in seeing the personal property of a family that was brutally murdered were fairly uninspiring. The one thing that had truly caught my eye was the old trunk jammed beneath the shelves in the shed. Franki's daughters, Kimi and Kylie, had mentioned that it was thought to be a hope chest for the eldest Hawkworth daughter. But no one had ever broken open the lock to confirm it. Another conversation popped into my head. Dash had talked about Garth, the boy who had been infamously known for breaking locks and propagating secret teen hideouts. He'd made particular mention of the Hawksworth Manor. I'd planned on waiting until one of the rare pre-summer tourist season weekends for the town to open the shed to visitors. I was hoping to inspect the trunk for a secret key compartment. But the night was still young and the idea of a walk sounded pleasant.

I grabbed a flashlight and my sweater and headed out on my adventure. If the legend of Garth was true, then it was entirely possible that the lock on the gardener's shed had long since been compromised. If that were the case, I relished the idea of a few minutes alone with the hope chest. There was more than a good chance that the chest had no secret key compartment, but if it did, it would be well worth the hike up to the manor.

I turned left off my street, Loveland Terrace, and up Myrtle Place. As I rounded the corner, I noticed a car parked several blocks down. Cars were rarely parked along Myrtle Place, especially at night. There were a few lights on the street, but there were plenty of shadows, all created by the plush Crape Myrtle trees lining both sides of the road. The distance and darkness and my lack of interest in cars made it impossible for me to recognize the make and model. I continued up the hill to the Hawksworth Manor. The great gothic silhouette of the house looked like a black paper cut out against the softly moonlit night sky. I rounded to the side of the lot where the gardener's shed sat tucked in its lonely, dark corner. The lights from the city were blocked by the massive house, and the moonlight got tangled up in some of the overgrown trees. The site was eerily quiet and nothing made me more edgy than darkness. I flicked on the flashlight. Its yellow beam spread out over the lot.

The barn shaped shed, original to the site, had been maintained by the town. While tourists were not allowed into the manor, with its crumbling staircases and ceilings, the gardener's shed was opened for visitors on special occasions and summer weekends. Port Danby had to make sure the building remained safe for guests.

I pointed my flashlight at the large, unwieldy padlock that gripped the latch on the sliding door. It certainly looked secure. I reached for it, certain that I'd wasted a trip up the hill, but as I pulled, the lock dropped open. I illuminated the top of the lock with my flashlight. It was hard to see clearly, but it seemed some clever prankster, probably even the infamous Garth, had jammed a tiny ball of paper into the hole, making it impossible for it to be locked tightly. Yet, when it was set just right, it looked as if it was firmly secured. I wondered if it was a rite of passage for teens in the area to learn about the various broken locks. What was more amazing to think about was that through the years, no one had given away the secrets.

I held the flashlight between my knees, so I could use both hands to slide open the barn door. An empty potato chip bag fluttered out through the newly opened doorway and bounced off toward the road. A crackling sound startled me. I circled the light beam around the yard behind me. The potato chip bag continued on its journey. It was hard to match up the sound I'd heard with an empty bag. I reasoned it away as a critter of some kind in the shrubby brush lining the property.

I'd been in the shed only once, but I knew that the chest was right near the door. I was thankful that I didn't need to journey farther into the room. With only my flashlight to illuminate the objects, the shadows and silhouettes looked especially creepy.

I didn't want to linger long in the building. I got right to work searching the trunk for a secret key. I knelt down on the thin layer of grit covering the wood floor of the shed. The miniature lock would need a specially crafted key. I was sure one of the reasons the trunk had never been opened was because the museum curators didn't want to damage it. And if the chest only contained linens and bed sheets, they would hardly be worth the effort.

I pulled the box forward. For a fairly good sized chest, it wasn't dramatically heavy, lending support to the bed linen theory.

Other than four nicely shaped squat feet, the chest was fairly plain. No initials or designs had been carved into it, which made me wonder if it was a hope chest at all. I used every yoga stretch I knew to feel along the back and sides. There were no secret compartments.

To get a look underneath, I had no choice except to stretch out on my side. I aimed the flashlight beneath the chest. The short legs provided only a three inch gap and the light did nothing more than allow me to check for spiders and mice before I slid my hand underneath. My bravery paid off. My fingers slid along the smooth bottom of the chest until they were abruptly stopped by an edge. It took some Twister game style moves, but I managed to find a latch. I pushed and pulled, something I'd learned to do when replacing the batteries on the remote. Without too much effort, a small rectangle of wood dropped onto my palm. Something metal slid through my fingers and clinked on the floor. I picked it up and held it under the beam of my flashlight. It was a very delicate brass key.

For the briefest second, a shadow fell across the room. I pushed up quickly to my knees and circled my flashlight around like the lantern in a lighthouse. I saw nothing and was too excited about my key discovery to pursue it any further.

I propped the flashlight on the floor to spotlight the lock. Surprisingly, with all the rust and years of being unopened, the key slipped in easily and turned with one click. I unhooked the lock. The heavy lid of the chest took slightly more effort than the lock. It creaked with age as I lifted it open. Mildew and dust from a long past era drifted up from the contents, causing my nose to itch. I rubbed away the tingling sensation and gazed into the cedar lined box.

It seemed the chest had not belonged to the eldest daughter but rather to the man of the house, Bertram Hawksworth. A stack of black ascot ties and three straw boaters, each one frayed from decay, sat upon a stack of what appeared to be business ledgers or account books. As I reached inside to pull one out, another shadow passed through the room. It had come from the open doorway.

The sound of receding footsteps sent my heart several beats ahead. I lowered the lid on the chest and pushed it back, taking care to snap the lock back into place. I slipped the key into my pocket for another time. Again, the creeping sensation that someone had been watching me crawled up my neck. I rubbed away the gooseflesh and got to my feet.

I lifted the flashlight, deciding with its four pack of batteries it could do some damage if I needed to wield it as a weapon. I hoped that wouldn't be necessary. I was more or less convinced that the noise and shadow had been caused by some teens coming up to the site to hang out.

I circled the yard with my light and saw no sign of anyone. Still, it was time to head home. I'd found what I came for, the key to the chest. And I was sure with some extra time and preferably warm daylight, I could ferret out some interesting clues into Bertram Hawksworth's life.

I slid closed the door and pushed shut the useless lock. I wasn't going to waste time listening for noises or watching for unexplained shadows. My feet started at a jog and then broke into a full run. I didn't stop until I reached Loveland Terrace and my cozy, safe house.

CHAPTER 28

*R*yder and I had been hard at work making pre-ordered flower arrangements. There had been so much to do, we'd barely had time to take a breath, let alone carry on a conversation. I knew it was going to be a brutally busy morning and decided to leave Kingston at home. He would, no doubt, be skewering me with angry looks all evening.

I tied the last ribbon on a bouquet of tulips and looked up and down the island at the array of finished arrangements. I lifted my hand. "I'm not generally a high-fiver, but I think this accomplishment calls for it."

Ryder smacked my hand. "I agree. I also think it deserves a couple of Lester's coffee mochas."

"Couldn't agree more. And tell Les to put them on my tab. My treat."

"Your treat for what?" Lola asked as she stepped inside the shop.

"How do you always manage to hear the last pieces of a conversation?" I asked. "It's as if you've got your ears primed and ready before you even walk inside."

"I do. After sitting alone all day in the antique shop, talking to Victorian dress dummies, I'm starved for conversation."

"I'm going over to get some mocha lattes," Ryder spoke up. His free, easy tone had disappeared. He swallowed hard before he asked about the coffees. Poor guy seemed to have no idea where he stood with Lola, and it was messing with his head. I wanted to flatten the black men's bowler on my friend's curly red head, preferably while she was still wearing it.

I was waiting for Lola to rudely dismiss his offer of coffee. Then she surprised both of us.

"That would be really nice, Ryder," she said in the sweet tone I'd heard her use often around men. "Whipped cream please."

"Whipped cream, right." Ryder lumbered out of the shop wearing a faint smile.

I stared at Lola as she fingered a few of the bouquets and then hopped up on her favorite stool. It took her that amount of time to realize I was giving her a pointed look.

"What?" she asked with a shrug. "I've decided you were right. I'm not being fair or kind to Ryder."

I took an excited breath and was about to jump into my list of reasons why Ryder would be perfect for her, but she held up her hand.

"You didn't let me finish. I'm still not convinced that we're right for each other. I don't want to start something that I have to stop in a month. Then I won't be able to walk in here without major awkwardness and tension. So tamp down the enthusiasm."

I began picking up fragments of stems from the island. "And when do you think you'll know for certain?"

Lola took the bowler off, shook out her curls and pressed it back down on her head. "I don't know, maybe about the time you decide that Detective Briggs is the one for you." Her brow arched up. "Or is it Dashwood Vanhouten that has caught your eye? Must be nice to have such choices. Tough too, I imagine. It's like trying to choose between a hot fudge brownie sundae or a box of chocolates."

"I think that bowler is a bit too tight on your brain." I dropped the stem pieces into the trash. "Oh, I nearly forgot. Your brilliant history lesson about hidden keys on antique chests has helped me on my quest to solve the Hawksworth murders."

"Did it? Good for me. What did you find out?"

I grabbed the broom and started sweeping. "You know that old trunk in the gardener's shed at the manor?"

She moved her chin in thought. "Not sure. Wait, that old hope chest?"

"Yes, but it's not a hope chest. And I know that because I found a secret key compartment on the bottom and I opened it. It was filled with men's clothing, accessories and some ledgers."

"Yep, that would be a pretty pathetic hope chest. Did you find out anything useful?"

"Not yet. A noise startled me. I closed up the trunk before I got a chance to really look through it."

Ryder returned with the coffees. He favored Lola with a gallant smile as he handed her the cup. She smiled politely back, and I thought he might fall over in shock.

Lola took a sip. "What was the noise?"

"Not sure. I'm not usually paranoid, but all evening, it felt as if someone had been lurking around watching me. Even when I was out in my front yard planting snapdragons."

"Sounds like you had a creepy night." Lola was occasionally expert at useless observations. "How do they get the name snap-dragons?"

I looked to Ryder, the human botanical encyclopedia. He was still recovering from Lola's sudden politeness. It took him a second to notice we were waiting for his explanation.

"Snapdragons? They were grown in ancient gardens. Their species name comes from a Greek term meaning 'nose-like'. And with a heavy dose of imagination the buds look like dragon heads."

"All I know is they're adding nice height and color to my garden."

"Now that I'm armed with more knowledge of the plant world, I need to head back to the world of old, dusty cast-offs and my headless, speechless friends, the Victorian dress dummies." Lola hopped off the stool. Her brown eyes sparkled as she looked at Ryder. "Thank you again for the coffee mocha."

Ryder couldn't find his tongue fast enough to say you're welcome. He just nodded his response. And I tamped down my enthusiasm but gave a silent cheer for my matchmaker skills.

CHAPTER 29

I'd sent Ryder off to lunch and had finally gotten the shop back in order when Detective Briggs walked through the door.

I had to practice some more of that tamped down enthusiasm. I was always thrilled to see him, but I certainly didn't need him to know that.

"Court time is over?" I asked airily.

"Finally. I've been back in town for a few hours. I wanted to fill you in on some details about the Letty Clark case."

"Excellent. I have something important to tell you too. You go first." I walked around to the customer side of the island. We were face to face, just a few feet apart, and I took a second to admire how especially handsome he looked in his dark gray suit and black tie. He always had to polish up extra spiffy for his court appearances, and I looked forward to seeing him in all his spiffy glory.

"The tech team was able to save Letty's phone and unlock it. There wasn't anything of particular note in the texts or call history. The last call was the one from her parents in Europe.

149

Earlier that day, she'd made a call to the phone number on the auction house business card. More about that in a minute." He stopped suddenly and looked around. "I wondered why I wasn't getting that creeping feeling I was being watched. Where's Kingston?"

"I had far too much to do today to keep my spoiled bird entertained so I left him at home. And remind me later to tell you about my creeping sensation experience last night."

Briggs' face instantly hardened to concern. "Did something happen? Were you in danger? I worry sometimes that I'm exposing you to hazards when you accompany me to interviews."

"Stop. It was fine. I wasn't in danger and please don't stop taking me along. You know how much I enjoy unraveling these murder cases."

"Sorry." He combed back his hair with his fingers. "I jumped right into hysteria mode, didn't I? I still haven't gotten past that scary incident at Christmas, when I thought . . ." His words trailed off. He seemed to shake the grim thought from his head.

"Trust me, I haven't gotten past that incident either. But it's fine and I'm here. So, what else have you found out about the case?"

He loosened his tie a bit. "The text exchanges with Darren Morgan sent up a few red flags. They seemed to slide back and forth along the emotional scale. Angry and hurt at times and then loving and kind the next. Their relationship must have been quite a roller coaster ride. Also, Letty's parents have arrived in town. They live in Chesterfield. They were, as expected, very distraught and not particularly in the mood for a lengthy interview. But they both seemed to go directly to blaming Darren for Letty's death. They said he had a bad temper and that Letty had been trying desperately to break off with him for good. But Darren wasn't making that easy."

"Wow, then it looks like you have a suspect. Or at least a person of interest."

"Quite possibly. Crimes of passion are common, and from the texts, it seems Darren was on the raw end of the relationship. He lives in Mayfield. I'm going to go talk to him later this afternoon."

"I see. Is your partner going to be involved in the interview? I could check out his skin care products. Men use hand lotion too, after all."

"I don't know. After what you told me a few minutes ago—"

"No, that was probably just my imagination. I was alone up at the Hawksworth site. It was dark and you know I get sort of wiggy in darkness."

A lopsided grin tilted his mouth. "I have witnessed you getting *wiggy* in darkness. But I think my next question should be—why were you up at that old house alone at night? It's not safe."

"It's a teenager hangout. It's certainly not dangerous either. Now that you've changed the subject completely, I'll bring it back around to your interview with Darren Morgan. Please," I said, using my most gracious, pleading smile.

"I guess you can go," he said with a relenting sigh. "You said you had something to tell me."

"Yes, I do. I nearly forgot." I pointed to his pocket where I knew he stored his notebook. "You might want to write this down. Yesterday, I went to Mayfield for some glass beads and ribbons. While I was waiting for an interminably slow woman to relinquish her highly sought after parking spot, I saw a woman walk out of Urban Antiques with a painting."

Briggs waited pen in hand. "All right. Is that all?"

"Of course not. The woman was none other than your favorite art teacher, Ms. Dean, and she was—" I paused for dramatic effect. "She was carrying the flea market painting that was missing from Letty's house."

He lowered his pen and looked up with full attention. "Are you sure it was the same painting?"

"Absolutely. Mountain lupines in an ornate wooden frame. She must have taken it from Letty's house. And that's not all. She looked angry about something when she walked past my car."

"Did she see you?"

I was surprised by his question. "Possibly, but I'm not sure if she recognized me. We've only met a few times. I'm hardly that memorable."

He stared down at the mostly blank page of his notebook and laughed to himself. "Understatement of the century," he muttered.

"What?"

Briggs shook his head. "Nothing. Continue."

"She was carrying the painting very casually. Then she tossed it into her trunk like she was dropping in a sack of potatoes. Not that I treat my potatoes rudely like that, but you get the picture."

"Got it. Do you think she was trying to sell the painting to Urban Antiques?"

"Well, partner detective that I am, I called Lola to find out a little more about Urban Antiques. Lola's parents are friends with Rick Urban. Rick used to work for museums, and he's an art appraiser. Jodie had come back to the flea market to buy the painting after she'd scoffed at the notion that it had any value. She must have changed her mind. Only I'm thinking her first instincts proved right, and the painting turned out to be worthless."

Briggs reached into his pocket and pulled out the business card. "I wonder if this auction house card has anything to do with the painting and with Jodie's sudden interest in it."

"Sudden interest enough to steal it?" I asked.

"Yes, I'll definitely be asking her about it. Good work, partner."

CHAPTER 30

"*I*'m on my way down to the police station, Ryder." I pulled on my sweater.

Ryder looked up from the sink. "Sounds good. I'm just going to clean up here, then I'll lock up the store. Have fun doing detective stuff."

"I plan to."

I decided to leave my car parked near the flower shop and walk down Harbor Lane to the Port Danby Police Station. The puppy's big gray snout poked around the corner of the station seconds before the rest of him bounded out on the sidewalk. Detective Briggs plodded behind.

Briggs ordered the dog to sit and after several forceful commands, the pup settled down on his behind. But his tail continued to spin wildly, like a tornado.

"I'm impressed," I said.

"With what? That my arm is still attached to my shoulder?"

I smoothed my palm over the dog's soft fur. "No. He sat. He's even still sitting." The second I said it, the dog leapt up to give me a warmer welcome. I rubbed his ears. "I guess you haven't found a home for him yet."

"A man who owns a junk yard off Highway 48 came in to see him. He was going to take him, but when he said the dog would just be out in the yard, guarding the property, I knew it wasn't the right home for him."

I pulled in my bottom lip to keep from grinning. "I'm glad you're at least being picky about his next home."

The puppy came back and sat right on Briggs' feet, leaning against his legs like a wall. "I want him to have a good home. Officer Chinmoor volunteered to watch him for a few hours while we're out and about. And I talked to Joseph Morgan, the auction house owner. I'll just get my stuff, then I'll fill you in."

I followed him into the station. Officer Chinmoor opened the counter gate and called the puppy to his desk. He opened the desk drawer and took out some dog treats. Briggs disappeared into his office.

I peered over the counter. "I think you should just keep him here as a mascot for the police station."

Chinmoor nodded in agreement. "I've told Briggs that a dozen times. We could get him a bandana with yellow stars, like sheriff badges. And we could name him something like Doc Holliday. Doc for short."

"I like that idea," I said, just as Briggs came out of his office.

"What idea?" he asked as he pulled on his coat.

I pointed over the counter at the puppy. "Doc Holliday, the new station mascot."

"I don't think so. I should be back in two hours, Chinmoor. By the way, I bought a new rawhide and some chew toys. They're in my office. Don't let him eat any furniture while I'm out."

I decided not to comment about the fact that he was out buying toys for the puppy that he had no intention of keeping. We walked to his car and climbed in.

"I thought we'd stop by Urban Antiques before heading to Darren Morgan's house. I'd like to ask Rick Urban about the visit from Jodie Dean. I called earlier to let him know we'd be coming by. I left a message for Ms. Dean letting her know I needed to talk to her, but she hasn't returned my call yet."

"It sounds to me as if you're opening up your mind to the possibility that Jodie Dean may be wrapped up in something nefarious."

"If she stole a painting from the victim's house, then I'd say yes. Even if she did used to let me out of art early to go to football practice." I knew the thought of his former, well-liked teacher being involved in a murder was a bitter taste for him to swallow. For his sake, I hoped the art theft incident was entirely unrelated.

"Have you been able to find out who destroyed Letty's artwork?"

"Not yet. My focus has been on her murder. However, I think we can assume a connection."

The morning had started with a handful of clouds, but the sky had cleared into a crystalline blue. We left Port Danby and headed into Mayfield.

"You mentioned that you had a conversation with the auction house owner?"

Briggs turned the car onto Parson Drive. "Yes, Joseph Morgan. He is Darren Morgan's uncle. Apparently, it's a highly successful auction house. Most of his clientele are extremely wealthy collectors. He knew Letty but not well. Joseph and Darren's father had a falling out some years back, so the two families rarely speak. He assumed that Darren gave his business card to Letty. He said Letty Clark called him on Saturday afternoon to make an appointment to see him. She said she found something that she thought might be very valuable. A call he'd been waiting for beeped through on his phone, so he had to cut the conversation short. But he told Letty he could see her on Monday. He was certain she mentioned something about a necklace just before he hung up. Obviously, he never heard from her after that."

As always, the parking spots on Parson Drive were filled. "Good luck trying to find a spot," I quipped. "We might have to circle the shops a few times . . ." My voice trailed off as Briggs pulled up next to the last parking spot and stopped the car.

He grinned smugly at me as he reached down for his red light. He stuck it on top of the car. "You were saying?"

"Well, if you're going to pull rank, then I guess rock star parking is always at your fingertips."

"Pretty much." We climbed out and walked down the sidewalk to Urban Antiques.

Urban Antiques was smaller than Lola's Antiques, but I had to admit (but never to my friend) it was more well organized. You could see every item and antiques were grouped somewhat categorically. All the clocks, ornate mantle timepieces, tall grandfather clocks and animated cuckoo clocks were arranged neatly in one corner, while another corner held shelves brimming with glass and porcelain collectibles. It seemed like an easier way to find a certain treasure, but I might have been wrong. It was more than possible people preferred a more mismatched, crowded antique store.

A man came out from a small office with two leather-bound books. He had smooth, dark hair that was graying on the sideburns. A black pinstriped vest was pulled over his white shirt. "What can I do for you?" he asked.

Briggs had his badge ready to go. "Yes, I'm Detective Briggs. I called you earlier about a case I'm working on. This is my assistant, Miss Pinkerton."

"Yes, of course. I'm the owner, Rick Urban. What would you like to know?"

"I have reason to believe that a woman brought a painting into your store to get an appraisal. And that particular piece of art might have been stolen."

His dark brows rose with the word *stolen.* "Guess it wouldn't be the first time someone asked me to appraise stolen art. Generally, I give them an honest appraisal. If it's from a well known artist, I quickly check to make sure it wasn't stolen from an art collection. But I must say, I haven't had a valuable piece of artwork walk through that door for at least a year. I had a regular client bring one in yesterday, but it was a fake. She wasn't too happy about it either." He stopped and his face scrunched up in confusion as he watched Briggs jot down a few of his comments.

Briggs looked up from the notepad, undaunted by the odd look the man was giving him. "Would that client happen to be Jodie Dean?"

This time Urban's full lips disappeared temporarily. It seemed he was trying to decide if he needed to answer. I was sure it had more to do with keeping a regular client than hiding something crucial.

"Again, anything you can add to help," Briggs said. "A young woman has been murdered. I'm working through evidence to find the killer. This is nothing more than a routine interview." It was hard not to admire how professionally Detective Briggs handled himself. He always managed to calm people's fears and suspicions with his relaxed demeanor.

"Yes, Jodie Dean came in with a mountain landscape." He laughed dryly. "I was sort of surprised. She's somewhat of an expert herself, and it was not a good quality fake. But she decided to have me check it anyway."

"Did she say where she got the painting?" Briggs asked the question that was on the tip of my tongue. Sometimes it seemed our minds worked as one.

"She said she picked it up at the flea market this weekend."

Briggs wrote that down on his notepad and flipped it shut. "Thank you very much, Mr. Urban. You've been a great help."

"Sure. Anytime. I hope you find the killer."

"We will," Briggs said. "Good afternoon."

We headed back out to the car. Several people were standing around staring at the plain sedan with the police light on top. They watched us with great interest as we climbed inside.

"Next Christmas, I would love it if you could drive me to the various shopping malls in this car. It would save a lot of time and angst not having to search and fight for a parking spot."

He laughed as he started the car.

"Where to next?" I asked.

"Let's see what Darren Morgan has to say about the texts on Letty's phone. And let's find out if he uses hand lotion."

CHAPTER 31

*D*arren Morgan lived in a small apartment on the second floor of a quiet building near the edge of town. He opened the door on first knock. There was no hello or attempt at politeness, but he invited us in without hesitation. He had pulled not just half but all of his long hair into a bun, and he'd jammed a long nail through the knot to hold it in place.

It seemed his studio apartment was also his art studio. We walked around several easels and a tarp that was covered with splattered paint. The paint fumes were minimal, signaling that he probably used a water-based product instead of oil.

"I've come back here with Miss Pinkerton, my assistant, for two reasons. The first one might sound strange but do you use a moisturizer on your hands?"

Darren had intense green eyes, which seemed to darken with the question. "I don't understand. Moisturizer on my hands?"

Briggs waved his arm around the room to remind him, unnecessarily, of his painting hobby. "Generally, people who paint have to use some kind of lubricant to counteract the drying effect of the paints and solvents."

Darren stared at both of us as if we'd just sprouted horns. Then, without a word, he walked to the door that led to a cluttered bathroom and emerged with a bottle of hand lotion. "Sometimes I use this stuff, but it's kind of greasy. I only use it when I've been working with oils and thinner, which is rare. Especially in this small apartment. The ventilation sucks."

Detective Briggs inspected the bottle briefly, then handed it to me. I put my finger on the pump but looked up at Darren first. The curiosity had multiplied on his face.

"Do you mind?" I asked before pushing the pump.

"Knock yourself out."

I squeezed a dollop into my hand and lifted it to my nose. I shook my head at Briggs. I handed Darren back the bottle and rubbed my hands together.

Darren stared at the container of lotion in his hand. "Got to say, I wasn't expecting this when you said you had some more questions. Would you like her to smell my shampoo too?"

Briggs brushed off the sarcasm. "No, the lotion will do. But I have something of Letty's." Briggs pulled the phone out.

Darren's face changed instantly when he saw it. But it wasn't worry or guilt. It was an expression of despair. "I bought her that phone for her birthday." His voice tapered off as if his throat had swallowed the words.

Briggs noticed the profound change too. It would have been impossible not to. He paused to let Darren collect himself.

"Mr. Morgan, there are a number of texts from you that seem, for lack of a better phrase, charged with emotion. It seems you were more than slightly upset about the breakup."

"Not going to deny that," he said. "I loved her and I still love her. If you're looking for someone who hated her, look no further than

Greta Bailey. That no talent couldn't stand the fact that Letty was breaking into the art world. She's the one you need to focus on."

"Have you been to Letty's house since her murder?" Briggs asked.

"No, it'd be like driving a knife into my heart to see all her things. All her artwork."

"Then you don't know who destroyed the paintings?"

Darren's face blanched. "Destroyed? What do you mean?"

Briggs put away his notebook, signaling that he was done with the questioning. "Someone took a blade to the paintings. I'm no expert, but I'd say they were damaged beyond repair."

Darren didn't answer. He held his jaw tight. Then, without warning, he spun around and heaved the bottle of lotion at the wall. It cracked open and white cream dripped down the plaster.

"Thank you for your time, Mr. Morgan," Briggs said. "And again, I'm sorry for your loss. We can see ourselves out."

We reached the door. "It was Greta," he said before we walked out. "I'll bet she destroyed the paintings too."

Briggs stopped and turned back around. "Then you need to let me do my work and put together a case against her. Please don't do anything that might put your own freedom at risk."

Darren's jaw loosened some. He nodded. "Just catch the fiend who killed Letty."

"I plan to do that very soon."

CHAPTER 32

*B*riggs was deep in thought as we drove toward Letty's
house. He decided to pick up a few of the ruined paintings and see if forensics could figure out what kind of blade had
done the damage. I could tell he was sorting things out in his mind
and I decided to do the same.

After the short visit with Darren Morgan, my intuition was
pointing away from him as a suspect. He seemed genuinely
distraught about her death, the first person from the art class to
show any real emotion about the murder. But maybe he was a
good actor, and my intuition hadn't caught the underlying deceit.
We'd definitely seen a display of the bad temper that Letty's
parents had described to Briggs. And a short temper can cause
even the most rational person to do things they regret. Like stab
someone in a fit of rage over unrequited love. Still, I'd seen true
heartbreak in the man's face. Then there was the more concrete
evidence that the hand lotion he occasionally used did not match
the one on the handle of the murder weapon.

I glanced over at Briggs. It seemed he wasn't ready to discuss his thoughts yet. We were both surprised to find two cars in the driveway of Letty's house.

"That's Letty's parents' car, and I think the sedan belongs to Jodie Dean. I hadn't told anyone about the destruction of the paintings yet. I didn't want to add to her parents' pain. Now I'm regretting that. Probably would have been less shocking to hear it before seeing it."

We walked up to the house. Briggs had kept the spare key, but it made sense that the parents had one as well. The front door was unlocked, but Briggs knocked first before entering. Jodie Dean was pacing the front room, clutching a piece of paper and occupied by a phone call. She hung up quickly when she saw us. Her face was splotchy red with rage.

She started waving the paper she held and shot me an angry scowl before turning to Briggs. "Detective Briggs, I'm glad you're here." She opened her mouth to continue, but her words were stopped by her phone ringing. She ignored etiquette and answered it.

Briggs looked somewhat irritated that she'd stopped in the middle of their conversation to answer the phone.

The sound of sobbing came from Letty's art room. Mr. Clark was comforting Mrs. Clark, a woman with the same baby fine hair and fair skin as her daughter's. Mr. Clark looked like a man who would like to tell jokes and laugh if he wasn't in a terrible state of mourning. He peered up first when Briggs stepped into the room.

"Detective Briggs, have you seen this? How could this have happened?"

"Yes, I knew about it. And I'm sorry I didn't warn you. I wanted to spare you some anguish. If you don't mind, I'm going to take a few of the canvases back with me to the forensic lab. I'm hoping to find out what kind of blade was used. It might have a connection to the—" He stopped short of saying murder weapon.

"Yes, please." Mr. Clark removed his arm from his wife's shoulder. "Please find out who did this. Her paintings were all we had left." That last sentiment raised another round of sobs from Mrs. Clark.

Jodie Dean, apparently finished with her phone call, marched into the room. "I can't find any art restorer willing to look at the paintings. Everyone is too booked up with museum work," she spit out the words with disgust, as if the restorers were responsible for the damage. I didn't know much about the art world, but it seemed she was exceptionally mad about Letty's paintings. That seemed strange because they had nothing to do with her. Or that was what I thought until she started waving the crumpled paper again.

"I have a bill of sale for three of these paintings, and it's worthless now," Jodie grunted with frustration. Her bellicose behavior was not helping Mrs. Clark's fragile state of emotion.

"Ms. Dean," Briggs said calmly, "I'm not sure if this is the time to fret about the loss of sale on the paintings."

"You don't understand," Jodie barked, "collectors were offering big numbers for her artwork, especially now that she's—" It seemed she had a sliver of decency left and stopped herself short of saying the word 'dead' in front of the grieving parents. Jodie threw the crumbled ball of paper across the room.

I saw that little tension twitch start up in Briggs' cheek, which meant his cool limit had been reached. "And I don't think *you* understand, Ms. Dean. Your rant about losing out on an art sale at this point in time is callous, and frankly, uncharacteristic from the Ms. Dean who taught art in high school."

Jodie's face darkened and her mouth pursed in embarrassment. It seemed the student had just put the teacher in her place. "I apologize, Mr. and Mrs. Clark," she said with a chill in her voice. With that, she turned sharply on her heels and walked out of the room and the house.

Briggs picked up the crumpled piece of paper and unrolled it. He stared at it for longer than I would have expected, then he pushed it into his coat pocket. We collected a few pieces of the slashed art and said our good-byes to the Clarks. On his way out, Briggs promised to find the killer and find out who'd destroyed the artwork. They were both too distraught to respond with anything more than a nod.

The shroud of sadness followed us out to the car as we quietly placed the destroyed paintings into the trunk. The one I had chosen was a painting of two little kids playing in a water fountain. Letty had captured the action and the joy of the afternoon perfectly. She had been a true talent, and to see the wonderful painting sliced open directly through the center of the fountain made my stomach harden like an apricot pit.

"What a shame," I said almost involuntarily.

Lost in his own thoughts, Briggs hadn't heard it. He reached up to pull down the trunk, but something on one of the paintings caught his eye. He lowered his hand and reached into his pocket for the wrinkled bill of sale. The paper crackled as he unfolded it and held it next to the corner of the fountain painting.

"Miss Pinkerton, look at Letty Clark's signature on this bill of sale and her signature on the painting."

I took hold of the bill of sale. "Scarlett Clark," I read. I lowered the paper to the painting. The canvas was signed by Letty Clark. "I don't think it's too strange that an artist uses a nickname on a painting signature. The bill of sale is a contract, so she used her legal name."

Briggs turned to me. "Yes, that makes sense, but if that's all you noticed, then I'm a little disappointed."

My posture straightened to meet what I perceived as a sleuthing challenge. "Uh no, that's not all I noticed," I lied. I held the paper next to the painting to survey the signatures again. Briggs waited in smug silence to see if I could find what he'd noticed, that I apparently hadn't.

After a few seconds, I sensed that he was about to tell me. I held up a hand to stop him. "Wait. Wait. Wait. I've got it. The capital C on the bill of sale has a curly cue at the top, like the way they taught it to us in third grade. But the C on the painting has no curl. In fact, it looks very different, like a backwards wave in the ocean."

"Well done." He took back the paper. "Of course, it took my prodding for you to look further."

I sniffled some with indifference. "If you say so."

We climbed into the car. It seemed his pompous moment hadn't ended. "I guess that's why they pay me the big bucks."

"Yes, well, you would only need to make a dollar to be paid big bucks compared to the partner on this side of the car. I do this voluntarily, remember?"

"True. Maybe we need to get you on the payroll."

"No, thanks. That would just take the fun out of it. Aside from my momentary lapse on handwriting analysis, do you think that bill of sale was forged by Jodie Dean? Was she hoping to profit from Letty's work?"

"The date on the bill of sale was intentionally scribbled, making it almost impossible to read. But I'd say that's exactly what Ms. Dean was up to."

"Then I guess Jodie Dean was absolutely not responsible for ruining Letty's artwork."

"That's the conclusion I came to as well."

"Greta Bailey?" I asked.

"That would be my guess, but the question is, did she also kill Letty?"

CHAPTER 33

I'd been so preoccupied with business and the investigation, I'd nearly forgotten that Dash and I had made plans to watch the full moon from the lighthouse. He'd been stuck working late on a boat that the owner needed fixed by morning, so I drove to the lighthouse to meet him. On my drive around the corner to Pickford Way, I noticed that Briggs' car was still parked in front of the station. A light was on, which meant he was probably working late on the investigation. There were a lot of puzzle pieces in the case, but none of them were forming a clear picture yet.

I parked a few blocks away on Pickford Way. I could see Dash's tall silhouette waving from the lawn in front of the lighthouse. I zipped up my coat and grabbed the thermos of cocoa I'd made for the moon watching.

We walked toward each other. "I came armed with hot cocoa. Thought you might need some after long hours on a boat."

Dash took hold of the thermos. "You read my mind."

We walked toward the lighthouse. The moon looked like a

massive gold button jammed in the middle of a blue velvet coat. "We hardly need to climb all those stairs." I tucked my hands in my pockets. "It's so big and bright, you could see it from anywhere."

"Are you saying you don't want to go in the lighthouse?"

"Are you kidding? I'm dying to see the view from up there."

The light keeper's house was dark. Marty Tate was most likely asleep for the night.

Dash yanked open the lock. "Yep, still the same lock." He pulled out a remarkably strong penlight and opened the door. The beam lit up the base of the tower.

"That is a penlight to beat all penlights," I noted as we slipped inside.

"Thanks. It comes in handy when I'm in tight, dark engine compartments." We walked up the squat steps to the long coil of stairs. Dash aimed the light straight up. Shadows crisscrossed the plaster walls. "Are you ready?"

"I sure am."

I followed closely behind him as we hiked up the seemingly endless metal steps. The walls narrowed as we climbed. "I wonder how often Marty has climbed these stairs," I said between breaths.

"Thousands of time, I imagine. Maybe that's why he's reached such a ripe old age."

"You might be right about that." I took another breath. "I think I'd just prefer to die younger than have to face this climb every day."

Dash's laugh echoed off the narrowing walls. "I think I'm with you on that."

We got to the top, but before I could enjoy the view, I had to fill my body and brain with the oxygen I'd depleted on the climb. Dash recuperated about two seconds after we reached the top, which was, to say the least, annoying.

"I don't consider myself to be unfit," I finally managed to speak, "but I think I need to start riding my bicycle more. I just climbed those stairs like I was dragging a fifty pound bag of bricks behind me."

"Maybe you're just tired after a long day of work." Dash scooted around the massive lantern to the front window and sat on the metal railing bordering the light.

I joined him. "Yes," I said too enthusiastically. "That's it. It was a long day, lots of flower bouquets and customers. I'm going with that explanation instead of the one in my head saying 'looks like you're getting closer to passing that threshold into your thirties'."

Dash opened the thermos and handed me the inside cup. He poured me some cocoa and filled the top cup for himself before replacing the cap. "Hmm, smells good." He lifted the cocoa. "Here's to a full moon, a lighthouse, cocoa and a sweet neighbor to share it with."

"Cheers." We gently tapped cups and sipped the cocoa. My gaze circled the panoramic view the wall of windows provided of the harbor and beach. "The world looks so vast from up here."

"I guess that's because it is vast."

"Good point. This is amazing though. Thank you for suggesting it. Did you finish the boat?"

"Finally. It needs an entirely new engine, but the owner doesn't want to fork over the money. Instead, I'm stuck putting little bandage fixes on it every few months. I told him with the amount of times he's had me come out to do repairs, he could have bought himself a whole new boat by now."

"His loss but your gain." I covered my mouth. "Jeez, I sound like a cutthroat business woman."

He laughed. "Not to me. You just sound smart. Which you are. Among other things."

My cheeks warmed, but I was going to blame it on the steam from the cocoa.

"So you had a busy day, eh?" He picked up the thermos and topped off our cups.

"Flower business is good. Especially with spring in the air." I stood up to get a better view of the wavy black water below. White crescents curled intermittently up and over in rhythm with the wind whistling through the lighthouse.

"I saw the tulip display in your front window when I went in to double check on our moon watch time."

I turned around. "You did? That must have been after I left. I'm working on a case with—"

"Detective Briggs," he added dryly.

"You know what's hard?" I said. "Being friends with both of you but having to pretend I'm not. I enjoy doing investigations with James, and I'm not going to apologize for it."

"You don't need to apologize. And I'm sorry we've made it difficult for you."

Dash stood up. Suddenly, the narrow space between the lantern and the windows felt extremely tight. I'd never been able to clarify my feelings for Dash. I truly enjoyed being with him and he was always charming. But I still thought of him only as a friend. I didn't think our relationship would ever go past that, and I was sure he felt the same way. Or at least I was until he stepped closer.

"Lacey, you know how fond I am of you." He took hold of my hand. It was the last thing I'd expected. Yet, I quickly started asking myself if I'd misled him by accepting his offer to watch the moon from the lighthouse. As his face lowered, a million thoughts went through my head, including one that seemed to say, maybe this was what you wanted, Lacey. Maybe you've been waiting for this kiss.

I had been waiting for a kiss . . . but not from Dash. At least not at that moment.

I turned my face and moved back a step. His usual confidence dissipated. It was the first time I'd ever seen Dash frown.

He pulled his gaze away. "I think we've both had a long day. Maybe we've seen enough moon."

"Dash," I started but had no idea where to go from there. "Yes, maybe you're right. It was nice though," I said to him as he turned away. "I think I'm just not quite sure about anything, but I don't want to lose your friendship."

He stared down at the water for a moment. "I understand. Are you ready for the long hike down?"

"Yes."

Without another word, he led me down the stairs. His dejected footsteps sounded extra loud in the hollow tower. This night had gone terribly awry, and I wasn't sure how to feel about it or how to fix it.

I was relieved when we reached the bottom. The fresh air revived me as Dash held the door open. He replaced the useless lock and walked me to my car. As I turned to once again apologize, he waved good night and walked away.

I would find a way to talk to him and explain my feelings once I knew what they were. I climbed into the driver's seat. "My thermos." I got back out of the car. The daunting thought of walking back up the endless flight of stairs nearly made me turn back. But it was a thermos my mom had bought me at Christmas, a vintage one she'd found in a second hand store. She had been excited to give it to me. She said it reminded her of the times she made chicken soup to fill my lunch thermos. I'd had the same wave of nostalgia when I opened it. I couldn't lose it.

I headed across the lawn. Dash had disappeared back to the marina where he'd parked. A few clouds had drifted in, landing directly over the moon and casting a shadow over the coastline. I stopped just a few feet from the lighthouse and stared up at it. I loved the lighthouse and the romance and adventure it brought to our coastal town, but tonight it reminded me of some ogre's tower where a distressed damsel might be imprisoned. Tonight, after the unpleasant incident with Dash and with the unexpected cloak of clouds, it looked daunting, almost menacing with its pointed black hat and small rectangular window eyes.

A shiver rolled through me and a creeping sensation raced up my neck. I reached back to rub it away and tried one last time to talk myself out of retrieving the thermos. But the memory of my mom's beaming face as she handed it to me coaxed me forward. I pulled out my keys and my own penlight, which was, unfortunately, a fifth as powerful as Dash's. But at least it would keep me from having to climb in total darkness. That would have been out of the question.

I reached the door and tugged on the broken lock. It didn't budge. I wrapped my entire hand around it and geared up to give it a good yank when an arm went around my neck.

CHAPTER 34

The arm bundled in a winter coat tightened around me. I flailed my arms back trying to smack my assailant, but I couldn't make contact. They yanked me hard, and I fell off my feet. The glint of a blade flashed by me. I screamed as loud as I could and clawed at the arm around me. My fingernails dragged across skin but my attacker didn't release me. In the distance and in my haze of terror, I heard someone call my name. I screamed again hoping I'd gotten someone's attention.

My assailant released me, but before I could regain my balance, the person shoved me hard. I fell forward. My arms shot out to stop me from slamming face first into the wall of the lighthouse. Footsteps thundered toward me, and a strong hand wrapped around my arm.

I screamed again and swung around with my clenched fist.

"Lacey, Lacey, it's me." Just hearing his voice made my body relax, but my heart was still pumping at full throttle.

Briggs' worried face came into focus. "James," I said on a release of breath before I pushed my face against his chest. His arms circled me.

"I don't see anyone." Dash's voice came from somewhere behind me.

I reluctantly lifted my face and left the protective arms around me. Both men looked gray with worry. It was hard to tell whose chest was heaving more from the race across the lawn. They'd both come from different starting places, but it seemed they managed to reach me at the same time.

The moment of terror had knocked me senseless for a moment, but as my head cleared, it dawned on me that they were both standing in the same place, just ten feet apart. Their few seconds of team spirit had evaporated, and the strained heat of tension seemed to fill the air around us.

"Did you at least get a look at them?" Briggs asked in a harsh tone.

"You're the cop, maybe you should have run after them. I'm not trained for pursuit," Dash answered snidely. "You were too interested in getting Lacey in your arms."

"Dash," I said sharply. I turned to Briggs. "James," I said with equal vigor. "Thank you both. I'm not going to complain about your tactics at all. I'm all right, but I think if you two hadn't shown up, I might very well be facedown on those rocks right now."

That statement caused Briggs to swallow hard. His breathing had caught up, but his face was still the color of ash.

"Can't understand why you didn't even get a glimpse," Briggs said under his breath.

Dash stepped closer. "Maybe they were wearing all black," he sneered between clenched teeth. "Again, maybe if you had helped with the chase . . ."

Both men had made themselves taller and bigger with chests out and fists clenched. I was still shaking from my attack, and their stallion fight was not helping. My stomach churned and I felt close to throwing up.

"Stop, both of you. This might have been a dream back in high school, having two guys face each other like roosters ready to draw blood, but it's not a dream of mine now. And if I didn't know there was some hidden reason behind this—" I waved my hand between them. "This cloud of testosterone, then I might be slightly flattered, but mad, nonetheless. So please stop." I'd kept my cool until the last words. A sob fell from my lips. I hugged myself to stop the shaking.

Properly chastised, they both relaxed their stances.

"Thank you both for saving me, but I'm not going to stand here and watch you two fight." I hadn't expected my legs to be wet noodles, and my first few steps faltered. Briggs' fast reflexes brought him to my side. He grabbed my arm to steady me and lifted my wrist to get a closer look at my hand.

"You're bleeding, Lacey."

From the corner of my eye, I saw Dash walk back to the marina, his hands stuffed deep in his pockets and his shoulders stiff with anger.

My legs solidified beneath me. I removed my arm from Briggs' grasp. "It's not my blood. It's from the crazy person who attacked me. I got in a good scratch."

"You did? That's excellent."

I shrugged weakly. "A little technique I picked up from my cat."

"No, I mean, that's excellent. It means we can collect DNA from the perpetrator. And something tells me, if we find the person who attacked you, we'll find Letty's killer too."

"Yes, I knew that." I'd been so busy recuperating from the harrowing experience, I'd missed the fact that I'd collected some irrefutable evidence right under my fingernails. I was going to have to give Nevermore an extra cat treat when I got home. And home sounded exceptionally good right then.

"Let me take you back to the station. I can swab the blood and tissue samples under your nails. Then we can get you cleaned up. Keep that hand still and try not to touch anything with it."

I looked around for his car. "How did you get here? In fact, how on earth did you know I was in trouble?"

He walked me to my car. "I'd taken the puppy out for a walk, and I saw your car parked by the town square. It worried me, so I put the dog back in the office."

"Alone?" I asked.

"Yes, hopefully the damage will be minimal." I handed him my keys, and he opened the passenger door for me. He got in and started the car. "I heard you scream and raced toward the light-house. Dash came down off the marina. He must have been working. Why were you out at the lighthouse so late?"

It was the question I was hoping he wouldn't ask. Which was probably silly of me because he was a detective. I was constantly dancing lightly around the truth when it came to Dash and Briggs, but I decided I was done with that performance.

"Dash asked me to climb the lighthouse and moon watch with him tonight. We'd finished and I was heading home when I remembered I left my—Oh no."

He looked over at me. "What?"

"It's just that I left my thermos of cocoa up in the lighthouse. It was a special gift from my mom. That's why I went back to the lighthouse."

"I'll get it for you tomorrow. So you had cocoa and a moon watching date with Dash?" It seemed he had cooled his heels some after the moments of angry tension with his nemesis.

"I don't remember using the word 'date' at all, but you're entitled to interpret it however you want." That silenced him on the matter. I was relieved.

We pulled up to the station.

"Anything else of importance you can remember? I know it's

hard if they grabbed you from behind and you never got a glimpse of them, but anything at all. An odor, maybe?"

I closed my eyes for a second to relive the horrifying few minutes. Then I opened them and looked over at Briggs. "Licorice. I smelled licorice on their breath."

CHAPTER 35

*I*t was late and the long day and now even longer,
crazier night made my head feel as if it was ten pounds
heavier than normal. Briggs was an expert at collecting evidence,
and he quickly swabbed beneath my fingernails to collect what he
needed for DNA samples. He had a special, disinfecting soap in the
kit made specifically for the purpose of washing up after acci-
dental contamination with someone else's blood.

His gentle hold of my wrist and intense scrutiny of my hand
and fingers, to make sure I had no open wounds of my own, took
some of the heaviness from my head and placed it solidly in my
heart. There was no way I could avoid thinking about how
relieved I'd felt when I was safely in his arms tonight. For a brief
moment, in his embrace, it seemed I was right where I belonged.

Color had returned to his face. The nausea in my stomach had
cooled to mild upset.

"What have you been up to this evening? This is late, even for
you," I noted.

"I had paperwork to finish up. I did have a visit earlier from Rhonda Diggle over on Culpepper Road."

"Rhonda Diggle? That's Fiona's sister. Fiona was the sweet, little lady who was selling the attic treasures, including the now infamous mountain lupine painting."

"Right." He led me out of the evidence room. "Would you like a soda or water?"

"A water, please." The puppy heard us in the hallway. He bounded behind us into the small, rather uninviting break room at the back of the station. Briggs just happened to have a treat for him in his pocket. He gave it to the dog along with a hearty rub before pulling two waters from the mini-fridge.

We sat at the break table, and the dog curled up beneath it.

The water tasted good. "Hmm, I guess being in mortal danger zaps you into dehydration."

Briggs shook his head. "I'm sorry that happened to you tonight, Lacey."

"You weren't responsible for the attack, James."

"Yes, yes I was. Port Danby is under my jurisdiction. And when I heard you scream . . ." His words trailed off. I was glad. I was still too much of an emotional eggshell to hear more. I reached over and squeezed his hand briefly, then did something I was expert at. I changed the subject.

"Why did Rhonda come to the station?"

"She was very upset with her sister. It seems Fiona sold all those family treasures without Rhonda's permission. And one item in particular—"

I sat forward and slapped the table. "So the painting was valuable after all?"

Briggs drew out the suspense with a long drink of water. It was hard not to notice how nicely his Adam's apple moved above the collar of his shirt as he drank. He put the bottle down with a satisfied sigh. "It wasn't the painting that had Rhonda in a fit. It was an antique doll."

"Oh." I sat back with disappointment but then sat forward again. "A doll? The same doll whose head I accidentally popped off? Jeez, I hope I didn't hurt the value."

"You didn't," Briggs said confidently. "Because the doll is not valuable."

"So it has sentimental value."

Briggs put his arms on the table. "No but it has a practical purpose. It seems Rhonda and Fiona's grandmother hid a very pricey necklace inside the doll for safekeeping. It was made by one of the big jewelers, Van cliff or something like that."

"There's an antique Van Cleef and Arpels necklace in that doll? My fingers were that close to a Van Cleef and Arpels? No wonder Rhonda was upset."

"So you've heard of it?"

"Any woman who has ever looked or admired a diamond has heard of Van Cleef and Arpels."

Briggs squeezed the empty water bottle. The puppy sat up so quickly, he bumped his head on the table.

"Just what you need, you goofball." Briggs tossed the empty bottle into the hallway and the dog loped after it. "So, if Letty accidentally popped the doll head off and discovered a necklace with the Van Cleef mark, she'd know she was looking at something valuable?" he asked.

It was easy to follow his line of thinking. "Absolutely. Which is why she asked Darren for his uncle's business card. Of course, the decent thing to do would have been to go right back to Fiona with the necklace, but I guess that hardly matters now. What happens next?"

"I think it'll be easy enough to find your attacker because they will have some noticeable scratches, but I'll need to request some

DNA samples from Letty's friends. We'll need irrefutable evidence."

I covered a yawn. "I'm so tired but I'm not sure I'll sleep well tonight. That attack shook me up."

"I'll follow you home and make sure you get in all right."

"Thank you. I'll take your offer." We got up from the table. The puppy was busy crunching the water bottle in the hallway. It took a short game of tug of war for Briggs to pull it away from him.

"What about calling him Brutus?" I suggested.

"Or we could let his eventual new family name him," Briggs countered.

CHAPTER 36

I sat up from a restless night's sleep. My neck was sore from being wrenched by my attacker. I had a feeling the entire incident was going to stay with me for awhile, including their bitter, licorice scented breath.

I climbed out of bed like a ninety-year-old woman and looked longingly back at my warm sheets and soft pillow. They beckoned me back with their cradling comfort, but I had a busy day ahead. I had planned to get to the shop two hours before opening to get caught up on paperwork. Yesterday, that had seemed like a sound plan, but this morning, with the way I was feeling, it seemed overly ambitious.

I walked to Kingston's cage and pulled the cover off. He roused with a stretch of his wings but then curled back into a sleep ball with beak tucked under wing.

"Yep, King, that's how I'm feeling too."

I tromped to the kitchen while avoiding tripping on Nevermore, who was circling my ankles with each plodding step. "No,

Never, I haven't forgotten that you need breakfast. You wouldn't let me forget that."

I reached into the cupboard for a can of cat food and knocked a box of cookies off the shelf. I pushed them back up to their place. As I drew my hand away from the box, I sucked in a breath. "Cookies," I said the word quietly, but Kingston heard every magical syllable. He began his cookie dance along his perch.

I quickly gave him a treat and filled Nevermore's bowl. Then I searched around for my phone, a feat that took longer than I expected. My night had left me so out of it, I'd somehow managed to leave my phone on the bathroom vanity.

My fingers raced over the screen as I texted Detective Briggs. "I know who attacked me."

A chill ran through me as I briefly relived the frightening attack.

"Good morning to you too," he texted. "Care to fill me in on the name?"

"Nope, you're the lead detective. You figure it out from the one clue I gave you last night. Licorice."

There was a long pause, then . . . "Your attacker works at a candy store?"

"Argh," I growled and rang him up.

"Good morning again." It was much nicer hearing his good morning than reading it. "So licorice, eh?"

"Yes, licorice."

Another long pause. "Licorice?" He asked again.

I laughed and groaned when my neck reminded me it was still sore.

"Are you all right?" His light, teasing tone vanished.

"Fine. Just sore. Like I was in a fender bender. And you're stalling. I'll give you another big hint."

"Good idea. And hopefully it will lead me to Jodie Dean."

"Darn. How did you know without my tell all clue of licorice?

Which, by the way, is the scent of Italian anise cookies. Like the ones your favorite teacher enjoys eating."

"Just a detective's hunch and a lot of connected dots. We both saw all the past due notices on her table. She was in financial trouble. She found out that Letty had asked Darren for his uncle's card. She must have decided that painting was valuable after all. When that didn't pan out, she forged a signature on the bill of sale of Letty's artwork. She knew that the paintings had gone way up in value once Letty was dead. A death that happened at Jodie Dean's hands."

"Well, all right, but I think my line to the suspect was much simpler and shorter. Are you going to arrest her?"

"Chinmoor and I are going to head over to her house right now."

"Uh, what about your other partner?"

He hesitated. "I don't know, Lacey. You just went through an ordeal, and it could be dangerous. Ms. Dean is not the thoughtful art teacher I had back in high school. She's a murderer and her last attack was on you."

"Exactly, and I want to know why."

"Fine. I'll swing by and pick you up."

I rushed through my morning routine and decided to skip the coffee. Briggs pulled into the driveway and I hurried out, not even giving him time to get out of the car.

"You are more energized than I expected this morning," Briggs said as he pulled out onto Myrtle Place.

"Guess it's the adrenaline caused by solving a murder."

"It's not solved yet, but I think we're pretty close. Officer Chinmoor is just waiting for a backup car from Mayfield. I need to have a female officer along for the arrest."

"Then there will be an arrest?" I asked.

"I think so. I'm going to ask Ms. Dean to show me her arms to check for scratches first."

"It's cute how you still use Ms. Dean like you're talking about your teacher."

"Good point. If she is our suspect, then she hardly deserves that level of respect." He lifted his coffee out of the cup holder and took a sip.

He caught me breathing in the scent of it.

I smiled. "I didn't have time to brew a pot and I was hoping I could get a little lift just from the aroma."

Briggs laughed. "Did it work?"

"Unfortunately not. Especially after last night. I hardly slept a wink. I can still feel that wretched woman's arm around my neck. She must have been the person who was watching me when I was up at the Hawksworth Manor." A shiver shook me. "That could have ended badly because there wouldn't have been anyone around to hear me scream."

He shook his head. "You've got to stop going up there alone at night."

"No lectures this morning, partner. We're about to crack a case. What I don't get is—why did she want me dead?"

Briggs turned onto Highway 48. The morning commuters were just heading to their jobs in Chesterton so the traffic was heavier than usual. "I've given that some thought. My guess is that she recognized you when you spotted her carrying the stolen painting out of Urban Antiques. She wanted to make sure you didn't tell anyone. She either lost her nerve or got scared off that night up at the manor, so she gave it another try."

"And almost succeeded," I said quietly. "While I got ready this morning, I was going over our first visit to Jodie's house. She was telling us about the prescription strength lotion her doctor gave her. I think she had just started using it because her hands were raw and red. I'll bet she has the lotion from the knife handle in her bathroom or somewhere in the house."

"Good point. I'll make sure the team searches for it. We'll need that. The DNA evidence will prove she attempted murder on you, but we'll need more for the actual murder trial."

Briggs slowed as he reached Jodie's street. "I want you to stay in the car."

"What? Really? But I skipped coffee and everything." A movement outside caught my attention. "Uh, I guess I can watch from here."

Briggs turned his face to the house and opened the car door. Jodie had a duffle bag in her hand. When she saw Detective Briggs walk toward her with his badge, she threw the bag and took off at a run. Briggs caught her in three long strides.

Officer Chinmoor and the backup cruiser turned the corner right then.

I climbed out of the car as Jodie Dean was being read her rights. Her face was like stone as she turned my direction. "I knew you were out to get me," she sneered. "Following me to the antique shop like you did."

I looked down at her arms that were bound behind her back. My fingernails had left three deep scratches on the back of her hand.

Briggs walked back to his car. "They're going to take care of things from here. I should get you to Lester's shop. You look like you're fading fast from lack of coffee. Since you helped solve the case, it'll be my treat."

"And a blueberry muffin from Elsie's? I skipped breakfast too."

"And a blueberry muffin from Elsie's. But first I've got to stop by Letty's house and pick up a doll."

"Oh my gosh, can I wear the necklace back to Port Danby? I've never even touched a Van Cleef and Arpels."

"I suppose you earned it. As long as I don't have to wrest it off of you once we get back to town."

"I promise I'll hand it right back . . . after a few selfies."

CHAPTER 37

"Friday at last," Ryder said as he grabbed his coat off the hook. "Some friends of mine are heading into Mayfield to go dancing."

"Have fun." I was wiping down the work station as he walked out. I hadn't heard anyone walk in when I turned back to my task. As I squeezed out the sponge, something pushed at the back of my leg.

I gasped, spun around and threw the wet sponge. It bounced off Detective Briggs' coat, leaving a large wet mark. He watched it fall to the floor. Before he could pick it up, the puppy raced over and grabbed the sponge. A tug of war followed which resulted in me having not one but two sponges.

Briggs held up both pieces. "Guess Bear and I owe you a sponge."

"Bear?" I asked excitedly. "You named him?"

"Yes, I didn't want to use Yogi because there was only one Yogi. But I thought Bear would be sort of a tribute to Yogi. You know, Yogi Bear."

I hugged the dog. "I love it and I love that you're keeping him. What made you change your mind?"

"A family came into the police station to adopt him, and they had an annoying ten-year-old boy who kept pulling on Bear's ear. And I knew there was no way I could send him home with an ear puller. Plus, Hilda came up and muttered in my ear that if I sent the dog home with the bratty kid she would never bring me fried chicken and mashed potatoes again."

"Then you had no choice."

"Nope. I'm sure I'll regret it about as much as I'll be glad about it."

"I'm sure." I dried my hands. "I think dogs should come with a warning label that says, I will chew up some of your prized possessions. I'll digs holes in your yard. But I will love you unconditionally, even when you yell at me."

Briggs patted Bear. I knew a strong bond had already formed between them long before Brigg's had decided to keep him.

"Thought you'd be interested," Briggs said. "Greta came into the station sobbing with guilt. She confessed to ruining all of Letty's paintings. Not a surprise, of course."

"It's amazing how crazy envy and jealousy can make someone."

Briggs reflected on my statement for a touch longer than I would have expected before a agreeing. "Yes, it is." He smiled. "Anyhow, I wanted to thank you for your help with the case and ask you one more favor."

"Anything."

"It seems I'm a new dad. I could use some help at the pet store finding things that will keep this four legged wrecking crew from destroying the house and the station and anything else in his path."

"I'd be happy to help you with that, Detective Briggs."

"Thank you, Miss Pinkerton." He flashed his best smile, the one that was a little crooked and made him even more handsome. "Thank you, Lacey."

MORE PORT DANBY

There will be more books in the Port Danby Cozy Mystery Series. I'm currently working to finalize the upcoming release dates.

Be sure to follow me on Facebook, (www.facebook.com/londonlovettwrites) and subscribe (www.londonlovett.com) to my newsletter and you'll be the first to know any new announcements!

DEATH IN THE PARK

While you're waiting for the next Port Danby release, be sure to check out my fun new series Firefly Junction. Book 1 is now available! Start reading on Amazon today . . .

LUSCIOUS LEMON CUPCAKES

View the recipe online: www.londonlovett.com/recipe-box

Luscious Lemon
CUPCAKES

Ingredients:

1 1/2 cups all-purpose flour
1 1/2 tsp baking soda
1/4 tsp salt
2 eggs
2/3 cup granulated sugar
1 1/2 sticks (3/4 cup) butter, melted
2 tsp vanilla
1/2 cup milk
1 1/2 tsp lemon zest
3 Tbsp lemon juice

Frosting:

1 1/2 cup powdered sugar
1/2 cup butter, softened
1 Tbsp milk
1 Tbsp lemon juice
1-2 drops yellow food coloring (optional)

Directions:

1. Pre-heat oven to 350°.

2. In a medium bowl, whisk together flour, baking soda and salt.

3. In a large bowl, beat the 2 eggs and 2/3 cup granulated sugar with a whisk or mixer until the mixture becomes light and foamy--this will take a few minutes. Gradually add in the melted butter and vanilla and mix until combined.

4. Add 3 Tbsp of lemon juice, and 1 1/2 tsp lemon zext to the wet ingredients and stir in.

5. Slowly add the dry flour mixture to the large bowl of wet ingredients. Mix slowly, adding half of the flour first. Pour 1/2 cup milk in and then add the rest of the flour mixture. Mix until just combined, don't overmix the batter.

6. Prepare a muffin tin with cupcake liners. Fill each cup about 2/3 full with batter.

7. Bake for 18-20 minutes. Test the cupcakes with a toothpick--when the toothpick is inserted in the center of a cake and comes out clean they are done.

8. Allow cupcakes to cool completely before frosting.

9. Make the frosting:
    -Add softened butter to a medium sized bowl. Using an electric mixer beat the butter until creamy.
    -Add powdered sugar in slowly about 1/2 cup at a time and mix.
    -Add 1 Tbsp milk and 1 Tbsp lemon juice, and a drop or two of yellow food coloring. Mix on medium/high until you get a good frosting consistency. You can adjust the consistency slightly if you want by adding a bit more powdered sugar or milk.

10. Enjoy!

ABOUT THE AUTHOR

London Lovett is the author of both the Port Danby and Firefly Junction Cozy Mystery series. She loves getting caught up in a good mystery and baking delicious new treats!

Join London Lovett's Secret Sleuths!
www.facebook.com/groups/londonlovettssecretsleuths/

Subscribe to London's newsletter to never miss an update.

https://www.londonlovett.com/
londonlovettwrites@gmail.com

Printed in the USA
CPSIA information can be obtained
at www.ICGtesting.com
LVHW042149230724
786338LV00030B/566